BULLION AND OLD BRASS

John and Fluff are on a quiet caravanning holiday in Wales with their Uncle Charles. But from the moment they glimpse a shadowy, mysterious figure at a deserted farmhouse, the quiet holiday turns into a tense adventure!

Who is the mysterious stranger? Is Caradoc Evens *really* going straight now? Who is the beautiful Leonie? Is she *really* just an artist? And above all, where is that £25,000-worth of gold bullion, still missing after it had been stolen so many years before?

BULLION AND OLD BRASS

The Cader Idris Adventure

by

Edgar Newman

Illustrated by Jacqueline Tettmar

JOHN GOODCHILD PUBLISHERS
WENDOVER

First published June 1979

John Goodchild, Publishers
70 Carrington Crescent,
Wendover, Buckinghamshire

ISBN 0 903445 54 9

Printed in Great Britain by
Hunt Barnard Printing Ltd, Aylesbury, Bucks.

Contents

Foreword and Dedication

Many books state plainly and rather sadly that they are works of fiction, and that the characters contained therein bear no resemblance to anyone living or dead. This does not apply to the book which you are now going to read.

Fluff and John are intended to be like every one of you who loves adventures and has a fondness for animals. It is to you that this book is dedicated.

There will be few among you who have not got an Uncle Charles of some kind or other, or who do not know a Leonie. As for Mr and Mrs Jones, there are lots of warmhearted kindly people just like them in Wales. On the other hand, the villains of the piccc exist only for the purpose of the story, and have no connection with any antique shop to be found in Dolgelley.

Dolgelley sometimes spelt Dolgellau, and pronounced Dol-geth-ly, is a real place, set in lovely countryside. Some of the place names mentioned can be found on the map, but Caffryn-Mawr, a little farm tucked away on the rugged slopes of Cader Idris, has been purposely disguised. Only a few really adventurous spirits will ever find it.

Now read on, and share with Fluff and John Carr their first adventure.

Edgar Newman

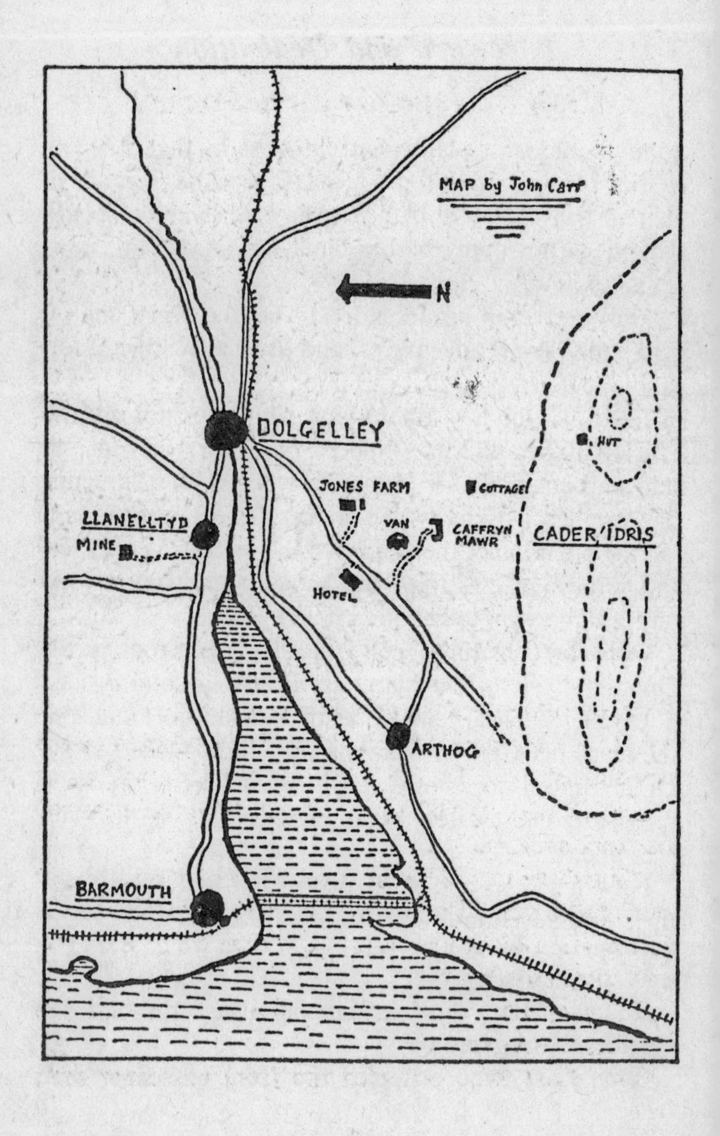
MAP by John Carr
N
DOLGELLEY
LLANELLTYD
MINE
JONES FARM
VAN
CAFFRYN MAWR
COTTAGE
HUT
CADER IDRIS
HOTEL
ARTHOG
BARMOUTH

Chapter One

Half a Mountain for a Pound!

Swirling grey cloud wrack hid the surrounding mountain tops from view. A gusty wind flung rain across the sky to spatter and rattle upon the car and caravan as Uncle Charles circled round to a halt in the deserted car park at Dolgelley.

"Shan't be long," he said over his shoulder as he got out of the car. "I'll just make some enquiries at the information kiosk over there, and then we'll be on our way to set up camp."

In a moment he was limping away through the puddles to the gateway.

John Carr, who occupied the front passenger seat,

turned to make a face at his sister. "What a stinker, Fluff, what an absolute stinker."

Fiona, better known as Fluff, grinned. "Well, it was you who suggested a caravanning holiday to Uncle Charles, wasn't it? And you even said we ought to go to Wales because you wanted to climb a mountain."

"I only suggested caravanning after you got chicken-pox and we couldn't go to Normandy with the school trip. It's your fault really, even though I do want to do a bit of mountain climbing!"

John, who was thirteen, and Fiona, two years his junior, were both at boarding school. After their parents had died in a car crash, Uncle Charles, then Chief Inspector C. D. Frost of Scotland Yard's Criminal Investigation Department, took them over and, as he put it, "Proceeded to drag them up in the way they should go, whether they liked it or not."

Since Uncle Charles was a kindly soul, not only did John and Fiona like his way of 'dragging them up', but they came to adore this grizzled giant of a man with a limp, who, shaken out of his comfortable bachelor existence, had made a new home for them at his Kensington flat, and made sure that at holiday times he was at hand to keep them company.

He soon came splashing back with water dripping from his disreputable-looking hat and raincoat, and by the way he was shaking his head the children could see that he had had no luck at the kiosk.

"Sunday afternoon . . . not a soul in sight, and as far as I can see, not a single shop open where I could make enquiries." He slid behind the wheel and wiped the rain from his eyes.

"What do we do now, Uncle?" asked Fiona.

"What do we do now, Fluff? Well, just as soon as I get my breath back again, we'll unhitch the caravan and leave it here while we look around for a farm with the right kind of site for us."

"Would this help at all, Uncle?" John began to unfold the one-inch Ordnance Survey map which he had bought specially for the trip.

Uncle Charles removed his hat so that the raindrops would not fall on the paper, and together they studied the area around the Cader Idris mountain range.

"Let's try this," said Uncle Charles, and with a pencil end he indicated a road marked in yellow on the map.

He traced the road on its winding way through a maze of close, red contour lines to where it joined the main road again at a place called Arthog.

"If we can find somewhere along there, we ought to be part of the way up your mountain, John."

They picked up the hill road on the outskirts of Dolgelley. It was narrow, winding and steep, but the big car, now free of the caravan, took it easily and they were soon clear of the houses. As she looked back through the rear view window, Fluff thought the sprawling town looked almost toy-like nestling in the valley below.

Quite suddenly the rain ceased, but the mists still hid the hills from full view.

Uncle Charles switched off the windscreen wipers. "Thank heaven for that! There just can't be any more water left up there I suppose."

Twice they pulled up and looked at possible farms. Neither seemed to have what Uncle Charles wanted. "We must have privacy," he insisted, "and we must have our own water supply close at hand."

"Do you mean a stream?" asked Fluff. "Is it all right to drink water from a stream?"

"Not usually unless it's boiled first," Uncle Charles replied, "but for washing there's nothing better in the world. You'll see – or at least I hope you'll see!"

This crack would have brought swift retaliation upon him had he not been driving. There had been a time when Fluff was not too keen on washing. The phase had now passed but was not quite forgotten.

As John burst out laughing, Fluff thumped him hard in the back. "You're not driving," she said, and hit him again even harder.

At that moment Uncle Charles drew up by a gateway on which was painted in faded letters, *Caffryn-Mawr*. "Let's look at your map again, John."

The map showed a road leading up to some buildings. It passed over a stream on its way, and two wooded patches were clearly marked.

"Shall we try it?" asked John.

"Yes. You look after opening and closing the gate, whilst I drive through."

The road, a rough affair consisting of two muddy uneven wheel tracks with coarse grass growing along the centre, wound round the hillside and disappeared from view in a clump of trees. The car bumped and lurched and slithered along until, on reaching a sudden dip and rise, Uncle Charles pulled up and said, "I think we'll go the rest of the way on foot. There's a van ahead, and I doubt if we can get by with the car anyway."

They set off with Fluff in the lead. There was no one in the van when they reached it, but lying on the seat was a wicker basket and thermos flask. This seemed to indicate that the owner was not far away.

Then Fluff gave a shout. "There's someone, Uncle!" She had reached a bend in the track from which the gate leading into the farmyard was visible. As the others joined her, they just glimpsed a figure moving rather hurriedly from sight among the buildings.

"Well whoever it was, Fluff, wasn't anxious to meet us," said Uncle Charles. "Let's push on to the farm-house."

As they drew nearer to the yard, however, it became apparent that the house was no longer inhabited. It was not derelict, but had that strange, forbidding look of an empty unwanted dwelling. Uncurtained windows stared out from it like unhappy eyes.

The front garden had long since surrendered to invading nettles, but the flagged pathway to the front door was clear. They went along it and peered through the dusty, cobwebby windows.

"There's still a telephone, Uncle," remarked John, "so the house can't have been empty all that long."

"Perhaps not," agreed their uncle, "but obviously there's no one living here now. Let's go back to the car and make some enquiries elsewhere. It's a pity, because a spot somewhere near where we left our car would make a fine site for the caravan; it's out of view from the road, and there's a stream not very far away."

"What about the man we saw?" queried John.

Uncle Charles shrugged. "Well, what about him? He may be just as much an intruder as we are. Still, we could try a shout, I suppose. *ANYBODY ABOUT?!!*"

They shouted three or four times, but only the wind

in the trees and the steady drip, drip, of water from a broken drain pipe answered them.

Uncle Charles turned in the direction of the car. "Let's go! There are none quite so deaf as those who don't want to hear, and our friend quite obviously doesn't want to hear us."

John and Fluff reluctantly followed their uncle back down the track. As they neared the car, they heard shouts and the barking of dogs in the distance.

Coming up the hill from the road was a man in a cap and raincoat, and in the adjoining field three dogs were busy collecting and driving the scattered sheep towards him.

A shrill whistle from the man sent the dog on the left flank into action, turning her charges towards the farm-yard gate. The dog moved quickly, crouching low in the grass with ears cocked, ready for each whistled command. She was ready too, when the sheep, in the awkward way that sheep have, tried to make a break in the wrong direction. It was then her duty to nip in smartly and set the leaders back on course again.

The children were fascinated by the scene. "It's just like a circus stunt!" cried John.

"Those dogs are far superior to any circus act, John," replied his uncle. "A good sheepdog is worth its weight in gold to the hill farmer. In this kind of country a dog can travel quickly in the most difficult places to seek out and herd his master's flock."

"I think I will be a farmer when I grow up," murmured Fluff dreamily. "Then I could have lots and lots of those lovely dogs."

To those who knew and loved her, this was not an

unusual reaction from Fluff. Animal mad, she regularly lost her heart to four-legged creatures of assorted shapes, sizes and habits.

As the sheep came closer they could hear the man calling commands to his dogs in Welsh. Soon they had their charges in position at the farmyard gate, a baa-ing sea of sheep. At this stage, one of the dogs, a youngster, left the sheep and headed towards the car. As he came up to the children he wagged his tail, wanting to be friends.

Fluff petted him. "Nice boy," she said.

"That's unusual," observed Uncle Charles. "This kind of dog doesn't generally take much notice of anyone or anything except its owner and the sheep it is supposed to be looking after."

There was a sharp call from the farmer. The dog pricked up its ears. The call came again. It sounded like, *Willybach.*

His ears cocked, the dog muzzled Fluff's hand once more, then, after a moment's hesitation, he ran back to the sheep.

"Willybach," repeated Fluff, "Willybach. I'm sure that's his name."

"Maybe," said John, "but I think he ought to be called Holdback . . . Holdback the Reluctant Sheepdog! I'm sure his mind isn't on his work."

They turned and retraced their steps to the gateway of the farm, still watching the skilful work of man and dogs. Uncle Charles made no attempt to interrupt what was going on, even when the noisy milling mass disappeared from view into the sharp drop of a small valley on the far side of the farm.

"It's better to wait quietly here until the farmer comes back to his van. He'll be much more ready to deal with us if we just stay in the background until he has completed the job."

It was, in fact, only a matter of a few minutes before the farmer and his three dogs reappeared. He closed the gate on the far side of the yard and walked towards them with the dogs quietly at heel. He was small, dark and wiry, with keen blue eyes, and smiled readily in response to Uncle Charles's greeting.

"Good afternoon. I wonder if you can help us? We are looking for a site for our caravan and hope you will let us camp near the little wood down the road."

"For how long?"

"About a week or ten days; it depends on the weather. We are willing to pay of course."

The farmer looked closely at Uncle Charles, and then at John and Fiona. Seeming satisfied he then asked, "You'll keep the gates closed?"

"Certainly we will." Uncle Charles produced two pound notes from his wallet. "May I pay you now?"

"A pound will be enough, thank you. If you would prefer to move up into the farmyard, no one will interfere with you. No one lives here now. It is a place I bought a year back, but I live at the farm over the hill."

Uncle Charles replied, "Thanks all the same, but I think we'll be all right near the wood, and there's a stream nearby which looks as though it would be suitable for us to use."

"Yes," said the farmer, "that's a good stream and quite safe. It comes from a spring just a little way up the hill."

Meanwhile Fluff and Willybach had been renewing their friendship.

The farmer leaned over to rub Willybach behind the ears. "My dog likes the little girl it seems." He grinned ruefully. "But he is not a good dog for the sheep; I know that, so does he, but he's a nice chap and I just haven't the heart to get rid of him. Perhaps he will learn better ways when he is older."

From the slight shake of his head and the playful cuff he gave to the dog, it was apparent that he had little hope of any real improvement in Willybach.

He was starting towards his van, when Uncle Charles asked, "Have you got anyone working here at the farm just now?"

The farmer looked rather surprised. "No, I have no one here. No one but me has been here since the sheep-shearing, when we used the buildings over the other side of the yard. But that was a fortnight back."

2

Uncle Charles told him of the mysterious intruder who had disappeared so quickly from view.

"He was an ugly man," put in Fluff.

They all looked at her. "What do you mean?" asked John. "You didn't see his face, did you?"

"Yes, I did; just before you others came up to me. He was looking our way and I caught a glimpse of his face. It was ugly and he had a beard."

"I don't know of anyone like that," said the farmer, with a puzzled expression. "If you see him again, perhaps you'll let me know. I do not want strangers of that sort hanging about here." He was looking at Uncle Charles as he spoke. "Some kinds of stranger do more than leave gates open. Many of us have lost sheep of late."

"Where do I find you," asked Uncle Charles, "if we do see him again?"

"My name is Jones, Gwylym Jones. You will see my house on the road back to Dolgelley; it is the one with the green gate on the right hand side."

"We'll remember. Now I must get our car out of the way to let you get by."

Fluff patted Willybach goodbye as he scrambled into the back of his master's van with the other two dogs, and then, with Uncle Charles setting the pace with his steady limping trot, they made their way back to their own car.

As they bumped back down the farm road, John said, "Do you know, it seems to me as though we have just rented half a mountain for our one pound note!"

Chapter Two

Old Brass

By six o'clock that evening the caravanners were firmly established by the edge of the copse marked on John's map as *Druid's Oaks.* The caravan was well out of sight from the road and snug by a shoulder of the hill. A row of trees by the track broke the winds which swept up from the valley.

John and Fluff, in wellingtons, had cleared away the bracken from the side of the stream at a part where a tiny waterfall rippled over some gaily coloured rocks. Then, with the spade from the boot of Uncle Charles's car, they deepened the pool at the foot of the fall, so that it was easy to dip and fill a bucket with the icy cold, sparkling mountain water.

Inside the caravan Uncle Charles was preparing supper. "Come on you two," he called. "Wash your hands. Food will be ready in five minutes."

That night they had bacon and eggs done to a turn, with mugs of steaming hot chocolate to follow.

John patted his stomach fondly, uttering sighs of contentment. "That was good, very good, Uncle Charles. I only wish I was an Arab so that I could show proper appreciation."

"What do you mean?" asked Fluff, intrigued.

"The young scoundrel means that he'd like to belch. And if he were out East, instead of being rude, it would be a means of showing appreciation for the meal," explained Uncle Charles, with a smile.

"Disgusting creature," said Fluff haughtily. "You get more and more vulgar every day."

"Off with you both," interrupted their uncle. "If you want to fight, do it outside! There's more room there; besides, I want to wash up. I'll do it tonight, but from tomorrow on it will be up to you two to wash up; my job will be the cooking."

John and Fluff pulled on their wellingtons again and went outside. "We're going to have a look round the old farm, Uncle," called John.

"We'll shut the gates," added Fluff.

"Don't be too long then, there's still plenty to do!" came the reply from inside the caravan.

Being a July evening it was still quite light, despite the grey clouds. As they walked up the track together it was just possible to glimpse some of the great crags of Cader Idris overhanging the farm, although the twin peaks were still hidden in the mists. There was a dampness of rain in the wind, and the sheep on the hillside kept up plaintive cries.

"I hope it will clear up tomorrow," said John. "I don't fancy ten days of this, although it's fun living in a caravan."

"Yes," replied his sister. "I want to go swimming, and Uncle says there are lovely sands at Barmouth just the other side of Dolgelley."

"And," John pointed up through the mist, "*I* jolly well want to climb that mountain."

It was strangely quiet at the farmhouse. Nothing moved anywhere. There was only a front door to the house and this was locked. The downstairs rooms, seen through the windows, were gloomy and creepy. Damp was causing the wallpaper to peel and hang in tattered streamers. An upstairs window was open, and John looked at it with interest. It could, he suggested, be reached fairly easily from one of the drainpipes.

But Fluff objected: "It wouldn't be right John. Let's see what there is in the outbuildings instead."

The lean-to next to the house had served at one time as a sort of scullery or wash-house. It contained a large brick-built fireplace, and, nearby, a great black iron cauldron suspended from the ceiling by a chain.

"Whatever was this for?" queried Fluff.

"Goodness knows, but it's been used fairly recently, I think." John prodded the ashes with a stick. "These don't look years and years old to me."

"Curious," said Fluff. "Very curious."

They explored further. Some of the farm buildings on the other side of the yard were locked, but one door opened to reveal signs of the recent sheep-shearing, with some fleeces still lying on one of the benches. In another building, a peep through the keyhole revealed a cattle byre with quite modern-looking equipment.

"Satisfied?" asked John.

"In a way," replied Fluff. "But I'd still like to know where that strange man disappeared to. I'm sure he is a nasty type."

Back at the caravan there had been an accident. While filling the water bucket Uncle Charles had slipped on the rocks and hurt his leg. He was strapping a plaster across a nasty cut just below his knee, when John and Fluff returned.

"It's this confounded lame leg of mine that let me down," he explained.

Just below the new cut was an ugly looking scar. "How did that happen, Uncle?" asked Fluff.

"It's the result of a bullet, my dear."

"But how did it happen?"

"Let me get my pipe alight and I'll tell you."

He shook down his trouser leg and settled himself comfortably. When his pipe was drawing properly, and all three were seated round the table, he asked, "Have you ever heard me talk of Buss Frisby?"

John thought for a moment. "Isn't that the man who got away from Dartmoor Prison last month and hasn't been caught yet?"

"That's the man. I put him there. But before that happened, and at the time I was making the arrest, he panicked and pulled a gun on me. It was sheer luck that the bullet didn't do more damage."

"What were you arresting him for?" asked Fluff.

"Robbery with violence. He and his partner, a man

called Caradoc Evans, were responsible for one of the cleverest bullion raids ever pulled. It took place in Lombard Street one New Year's Day. Evans planned it; he was the brains, while Frisby was the brute force of the partnership. After coshing two of the guards they got away with a van containing just over half a million pounds worth of gold bars."

"But you caught them, Uncle?"

"Oh yes, John, we caught them all right. But we only recovered half the gold. We always thought that was Frisby's share of the loot. He had it tucked away in a henhouse at his sister's place out Epping way. The two men were together when I made the arrest, but Frisby, fool that he was, took a pot shot at me; so he got fourteen years while Evans only got five. We tried to keep tabs on Evans after he was released, just to see if he would lead us to the missing gold, but he disappeared into thin air."

Here Uncle Charles paused, but after a few moments he added, "So now Scotland Yard are short of Evans, Frisby, a quarter of a million, and me. You see, it was largely because of Frisby's bullet in the leg that I got put on the early retirement list last autumn." A note of bitterness crept into his voice as he said, "Just as a matter of self-satisfaction, I would have liked to have finished the business and unearthed the last of the gold. I hate to think of that rat Evans living in luxury on his ill-gotten gains."

"Do you think he helped Frisby to escape?"

"I don't know, Fluff, I just don't know. It's more than likely, because he'd probably need help in shifting the gold. A quarter of a million in gold bars weighs quite a bit, and, as I said before, Evans supplied the brains not the brawn."

The next morning dawned fine. There was no rain, no wind and no mist. At eight o'clock Fluff woke to the sound of Uncle Charles getting breakfast. The sun was peeping into the caravan from over a flanking shoulder of Cader Idris.

"Come on lazybones," called John. "I've been up for hours."

"Ten minutes precisely," put in Uncle Charles. "Just time enough for a quick lick and a promise. But out you get, young woman, and get a flannel round your face!"

Healthy appetites made breakfast a quiet meal. As Fluff was putting marmalade on her second piece of toast, she asked, "What are we going to do this morning, Uncle?"

"After you and John have washed up – remember, washing up? It's your job from now on – we are going into the town for some shopping. If we all go, each one can get a share of the things we need, and then we'll be finished more quickly and can go off to Barmouth for a dip before lunch."

The washing up was swiftly dealt with, the swimming gear packed into the car, and about an hour later they were parking the car in Dolgelley.

Fluff's job was to get milk and butter. She soon found the dairy in a side street, and then, whilst waiting for the others, had a quick look in some of the shop windows.

One window in the main street intrigued her immensely. It was full of all sorts of curios. There were strangely wrought rings, gay trinkets, and row upon row of brass ornaments all gleaming brightly in the sunlight. Little Welsh ladies in tall brass hats jostled funny little men with brassy smiles. Some held ashtrays or matchboxes. Some were egg-timers, and some were brass bells. There were also letter-racks and door-knockers and every conceivable kind of horse brass. Over the door was written, *WELSH ANTIQUES*, and in smaller lettering, *C. Evans – Proprietor.*

"There's one sucker born every minute," said a laden John coming up behind his entranced sister.

"What do you mean – sucker?" retorted the indignant Fluff.

"Sucker! They make things like those in Birmingham by the thousand. They're no more antique than I am."

"I don't believe you," replied Fluff. "These are too nice."

"Quite right too, young lady: every one is a piece of real Welsh craftsmanship."

The voice from inside the open door was ingratiatingly friendly. The owner appeared with a pair of bellows in one hand and a polishing cloth in the other. "Look at this piece, my dear, just look at it. It came recently from a farmhouse in the hills. Real brass bellows, my dear, made more than one hundred and fifty years ago."

He rubbed vigorously and then, quite suddenly, disappeared into the shop. It was as though the bellows had been a Welsh substitute for Aladdin's famous lamp, and the too genial Mr Evans the Genie himself.

At that moment Uncle Charles quietly appeared on the scene.

"John's just had his silly nose put out of joint," gurgled Fluff with glee.

"How's that?"

"He said the things in the window here weren't genuine, and the owner heard him say it."

"So what!" John put in, unabashed. "I still don't believe it; well, not altogether."

Uncle Charles had rather a puzzled look on his face. He glanced up at the name over the shop door. "C. Evans," he muttered. "I wonder . . . "

They had moved away out of sight of the shop, in the direction of the car park, when he stopped abruptly and said to Fluff, "How much were those horse brasses in the window?"

"They were seventy-five or ninety pence, I think, Uncle," she replied, looking puzzled. "Perhaps more for the bigger ones."

"Here's a pound, Fluff. I want you to go back to that shop and buy any one you like. If Master C. Evans is careless, we might be very, very lucky. John and I will wait here for you."

It was a breathless and still puzzled Fluff who returned five minutes later clutching her change and a small brown paper parcel. When they got to the car, Uncle Charles unwrapped the brass ornament with great care, and holding it gingerly by its edges, examined the surfaces.

"Master Evans was careless then." He pointed to a smudge on the back of the brass. "This ought to be clear enough for the boys at Scotland Yard to check."

"What do you mean, Uncle?" chorused John and Fluff.

"I rather think the name over the shop should read Caradoc Evans, and that's why there was such a sudden disappearance when I came up the street," replied their Uncle, busy repacking the parcel.

Not long afterwards that same parcel, in a strong protective wrapper, and addressed to the Fingerprint Department of New Scotland Yard, was registered and in the post.

Chapter Three

Druid's Stones and a Painter

Despite continuous pestering, Uncle Charles flatly refused to discuss the matter of the fingerprint or Mr Evans any further.

As he pointed out, "I last saw Caradoc Evans in the dock at the Old Bailey. He was a young man then, and unmarked by prison life. The man we saw today was thin, grey and lined, and had only a vague resemblance to the Evans I knew. Evans is a common enough name, too. No, we mustn't jump to hasty conclusions. We'll just have to wait patiently for the experts to tell us whether or not the fingerprint on the brass matches up with their records. But remember, it may not even be *his* fingerprint. Anyone could have handled that brass."

So, for the time being anyway, Mr C. Evans, Shopkeeper, or Caradoc Evans, ex-convict, was a forbidden topic.

After their dip and a snack lunch on a quiet stretch of beach, they drove back to Caffryn-Mawr.

"Now what?" asked John.

"An hour on the bed for me," insisted Uncle Charles, yawning. "I'm feeling my years after that swim. If the pair of you have got the energy, I suggest you take a walk and trace our stream back for a way, just to make sure it is all right. I'd hate to think there might be a dead sheep lying in it!"

Fluff made a face. "Don't be horrid, Uncle."

John said, "That's not horrid, that's practical, so come on and look."

They followed the winding course of the stream, scrambling over rocks and skirting the bushes by Druid's Oaks. As they climbed higher, the stream dwindled to a narrow ribbon of silver, and finally they reached the source, where water gushed merrily from a small hole in the hillside.

"Well, that's all right," cried Fluff, panting, and with obvious relief. "There's nothing dead in that!"

"But there was once, in *that!*" John, who had his map open, was pointing further up the hill to a curious formation in the stone wall which bounded the field they were in and separated it from the copse.

Fluff, looking in the direction he had indicated, saw what appeared to be one immense flat stone resting on two other big stones. "It's like a small piece of Stonehenge," she commented.

"It's marked here as a Burial Chamber."

Fluff thought for a moment. "You know our wood is called Druid's Oaks on your map. Do you think these are Druid's stones?"

"Let's go closer and have a good look." John put his map away and was soon well ahead of his sister.

When she joined him at the stones, he was quite excited. "It really *was* a chamber. The top stone is resting on three wall stones, not just two, and it looks as though this other stone might have made the fourth wall."

"Do you mean somebody was once buried in there?" Fluff felt a bit uneasy.

"Yes, hundreds and hundreds of years ago."

"I don't think I like it," Fluff said, wandering off towards a small stone barn which stood in the corner of the field. "That looks more interesting; it could have been a cottage once. Besides, I'd rather look at places that people have lived in than where they got buried."

"Wait a moment, Fluff," called John, urgently.

Fluff stopped, and waited for John to come up to her. He held his finger to his lips to indicate silence.

"Look over there," he whispered, pointing to the side of the barn. "See?"

Half expecting to catch another glimpse of the bearded intruder, Fluff looked. "It's only somebody painting," she said, a little disappointed.

Either they had not been sufficiently silent, or their movements had attracted attention, for the artist was looking in their direction with eyes shielded against the sun.

"Do you think we could go over and look?"

"Why not?" Once again John took the lead.

As they got closer, they saw that the artist was a woman. Despite the fact that she looked dreadfully untidy with paint-stained hands and a paint-smothered blue smock, there was, Fluff decided, something rather nice about her.

John, in describing her to Uncle Charles afterwards, said, "Oh, she's getting on a bit; about thirty-five I should think, and has dreadful ginger hair."

Which was quite an inadequate way of describing the extremely attractive young woman, with a rich auburn mop, who had greeted them in so friendly a way.

"I expect you want to see?"

"May we?" asked Fluff.

"You may. But do remember, it's not finished yet."

The canvas was quite large. Taking shape on it was a picture of Caffryn-Mawr farmhouse and the crags and peaks of Cader Idris beyond.

"Not bad," admitted John.

"Fabulous!" declared Fluff emphatically.

"Such praise is praise indeed." She was smiling. "I suppose you are from the caravan which came yesterday."

John, as spokesman, said, "Yes."

"I'm staying with Mr Jones the farmer, and he told me about you."

"Gosh!" Fluff was bubbling with excitement. "Do you live with Willybach?"

"Mr Jones's young sheepdog?"

"Yes, Willybach. He's a pet."

John excused Fluff. "Fluff goes crazy over all animals."

"Well, Willybach *is* rather nice. And what does Fluff stand for?"

Fluff introduced herself. "I'm Fiona Carr, this is my brother John, and we are staying here with our Uncle Charles."

"And my name's Leonie Bretherton – Miss Leonie Bretherton."

"Are you a *real* artist?"

Miss Bretherton looked slightly taken aback, but she

had a very good sense of humour and recovered quickly.

"Yes, Fluff, I don't do it for a living, but I do exhibit pictures, and some I sell."

"Gosh!" said Fluff again. "May we watch you paint?"

"Not today, my dear." Miss Bretherton was already cleaning her brushes on pieces of newspaper. "The light is changing too quickly and the shadows are moving too fast. If it's fine, I shall be back tomorrow and perhaps almost finish it."

They waited whilst she packed up her stool, easel and box of paints. The canvas she put in the old cottage. "I don't suppose anyone will touch it," she commented.

Together they walked down the hill. "Come and meet Uncle Charles," invited John.

"I'd like to," replied Miss Bretherton.

But when they got to the caravan and opened the door, sounds of gentle snoring greeted them. Uncle Charles was sound asleep.

With a smile Miss Bretherton tiptoed away. "Don't wake him," she whispered. "We can always meet tomorrow."

Chapter Four

The Curious Behaviour of an Artist

After a big supper of steak and chips, the caravanners took a brisk walk down to the Gwernan Lake Hotel, a pleasant place which stands near the start of the Foxes' Path climb to the peaks of Cader Idris.

There was, as Uncle Charles had anticipated, a gathering of climbers in the lounge talking over their conquests of the day, and their hopes for tomorrow. Mingling with the crowd, Uncle Charles made enquiries about the possibility of John being able to join a climbing party.

"That's easy enough," said a bronzed, burly young man. "Tomorrow I'm taking a party from the Youth Hostel over the easy way and back."

He looked critically at John. "Has he got a stout pair of boots?"

John quickly answered, "Yes, I've got boots."

"Well then, all you'll need is something in a knapsack to eat and drink. You can meet us here just after nine o'clock tomorrow morning."

"What if it's wet, or too misty?" asked Uncle Charles.

"Then we'll go the day after."

With this settled, they returned to the caravan with John already on top of the world.

"Relax!" said his uncle. "Get out the cards and we'll play Rummy for a bit, and then it's early to bed for all of us!"

Fluff, who had a whole double bed to herself at the far end of the caravan, slept badly that night. It seemed too hot and stuffy, even though the partition, which made her part of the caravan private, had been pulled back, and all the windows were open.

She sat up and looked at the luminous dial of her watch. It read five minutes past midnight. Outside she could see only blackness, through which could be heard the sighing of the wind amongst the leaves of the oak-trees, and the gentle murmur of waterfalls on the hill-side.

Suddenly, the stillness was broken by the clink, clink, of footsteps, and she glimpsed, but only for a moment, the cone of light from a torch pointed downwards.

Someone was moving along the track towards the farm, and doing so with considerable caution. Twice the footsteps stopped, as though the intruder was pausing to listen.

Then the torch flashed again, but among the trees this time, showing a change of direction towards the Druid's Stones, as Fluff had named the ancient burial place on the hill.

"Whoever can it be at this time of night?" she asked herself.

At that moment there must have been a stumble, for to Fluff's keen young ears came the sound of an angry exclamation in a voice distinctly feminine. This was followed by complete silence.

"Miss Bretherton!" said Fluff to herself. "But surely she can't be worried enough about her painting to go up to the cottage at this time of night?"

It was a long time before there was any more movement, and Fluff lay back puzzled to await Miss Bretherton's return; but sleep comes quickly when it is not sought, and if she came back by the same route, no one in the caravan heard her.

It was another lovely morning, with a warm sun to gild the hills and scarcely a cloud in the deep blue sky.

"Who'd have believed it, after Sunday!" exclaimed Uncle Charles as he and Fluff waved goodbye to a rucksacked and booted John setting off to join the climbing party. "The view from the top should be marvellous today."

As they were clearing up after breakfast Fluff mentioned the late passerby. "I'm sure it was Miss Bretherton, and after I've washed up I'll slip up the hill and see if her painting is still in the hut."

The painting was still there when Fluff arrived at the old cottage. Moreover it showed no signs of having been moved.

Fluff studied the canvas. The more she saw it, the more she liked it, and the more she wished she had the same skill as Miss Bretherton. She moved outside to where the artist had been sitting. There she studied the scene before her: a meadow which fell steeply away, a jumble of farm buildings, and, high over the farm, the massive crags of Cader Idris. The scene was alive with rich colours and moving shadows. As Fluff looked down she could see why Miss Bretherton used blues and reds and greens instead of black for shadows. The shadows weren't black at all.

"I must remember that when I paint," she said to herself.

Suddenly, Fluff's attention was caught by a movement in the shadows at the side of the house. It was Miss Bretherton, and she seemed to be searching for something.

Fluff was intrigued; so intrigued that she could not resist the temptation to get really close to see more of what was going on. Taking care to keep out of sight behind a stone wall, she crept up to the outer range of farm buildings.

Leonie Bretherton had gone into the outbuilding where Fluff and John discovered the great iron cauldron. The door was wide open, and Fluff could see her poking about amongst the ashes in the fireplace with a stick.

As she watched, Fluff became aware of somebody

else cautiously moving towards the building from her left. Once more she had a tantalising glimpse of the bearded intruder. He, too, seemed to be interested in the activities of Leonie Bretherton, and, unaware of Fluff's presence, he very carefully worked his way into a clump of bushes by the sheep-dipping pen.

Fluff decided to transfer her attention to the man and moved quietly away to get a closer look at him.

A moment later her shrill scream went ringing out to echo and re-echo among the hills.

There are two things, Uncle Charles firmly decided, which spoil caravanning. One is making up the beds at night, and the other is stripping them down in the morning, and storing the sheets and blankets out of the way to make room for day-time activities.

Today was to be bed-airing day. After Fluff departed on her quest up the hill, he stretched some cord between a couple of trees at the edge of the wood, and hung the blankets out to catch the sun.

It was while he was putting out the last of these that he saw Fluff moving carefully alongside a wall near the farm. "What mischief is that young minx up to now?" he asked himself. "I think I'd better follow and find out. The stalker," he smiled, "is about to be stalked."

Just then Fluff's shrill scream rang out.

"Coming Fluff! Coming!" he cried, running as fast as his lame leg would allow.

But Leonie Bretherton had already gone to Fluff's aid. When Uncle Charles arrived on the scene, she had just pulled a very wet youngster from the deep, stagnant water of the sheep-dipping pen, and was wiping her face with a quite inadequate handkerchief.

"Whatever did you do, Fluff?"

Fluff spluttered. "I slipped. I was trying to get a close look at the bearded man, and I slipped on the edge of the dip tank." She then added unnecessarily, "I fell in!"

Uncle Charles and Leonie Bretherton looked at each other at the mention of the bearded man, but Uncle Charles said, "First things first, young woman. Perhaps Miss . . . ?"

"Bretherton. Leonie Bretherton."

"Perhaps Miss Bretherton will give me a hand to get you down to the caravan and dry again, and after that we'll talk about bearded men!"

Half an hour later they sat round the caravan table with large mugs of hot chocolate in front of them. Fluff, well washed, and towelled dry by Leonie, was dressed in clean clothes.

She made no mention of spying on Miss Bretherton, and concentrated on telling them about spotting the bearded man. "I don't think he's a nice man at all," she said. "After all, he was quite close and he could have pulled me out."

Leonie said she had seen no sign of the man and gave a very ready explanation of her own presence at the farm. "I work," she began, "for one of the big advertising agencies. I'm really here on a painting holiday, but I've been rummaging around the farm looking for old implements and tools which might make up into a photographic background to an advertisement we are planning for a new tractor. You know the idea – contrasting the modern, up-to-date piece of equipment with the old, out-of-date stuff."

Uncle Charles asked her if she had ever seen anything of the bearded man while she had been sitting on the hillside painting.

She hesitated, and then said quite firmly, "No." And then, as if to change the subject, "Do you realise that I've been calling you 'Uncle Charles'?" She smiled. "Do you mind?"

"Not really," he replied. "But I'd better put matters to rights by telling you that my name is Frost, Charles Frost."

At this, a hint of recognition showed in Leonie's eyes, and a touch of wariness crept into her manner. "Yes, Mr . . . " she paused. "Frost. I must remember that."

She got up to go, picking up her paintbox, easel and stool. "Thank you for the chocolate. I must be getting back to work again on my picture while the light and shadows are right."

"Thank you for helping me," put in Fluff. "I might have drowned."

"Impossible!" declared her uncle. "Only the good die young, and you'll live to a ripe old age!" He paused and became serious. "All the same, Miss Bretherton, I'm glad you were at hand to pull her out."

Leonie left them, and went off up the hill. Fluff said, "Uncle, I don't believe a word about that advertising picture, I just *don't.*"

"Nonsense, Fluff – it's quite a reasonable explanation."

Fluff picked up the three empty chocolate cups and put them in the sink for washing up. "You'll see," she said darkly. "You'll see!"

A few minutes later Miss Bretherton came back past the caravan. "It's no good," she called, "I can't make a start. I've run out of burnt umber, and I'll have to go into town to get some more."

Fluff turned to her uncle. "I told you so!" Before he could make any comment, she continued, "She's a fibber. Yesterday when John and I were watching her pack up her paints, I remember seeing the name 'Burnt Umber' on one of the tubes. It was a new tube, too, hardly used. I remembered the name because I wondered what colour it was supposed to be."

Uncle Charles asked, "Are you sure, Fluff?"

"Quite sure, Uncle." Then she suggested, "Let's go and have a look in her paint box. She must have left it up on the hill because she was empty-handed when she passed by just now."

They walked up the hill together to where the paint-box, easel and stool lay on the ground. The box did not appear to have been opened. When they looked inside they soon saw a large tube of burnt umber. It was nearly full.

Chapter Five

More About Burnt Umber

"I think, Fluff, we'll have a quick lunch in town today, then I can do some telephoning while you do the shopping."

Uncle Charles had brought in the fresh, warm-smelling blankets and was tucking them away in one of the seat lockers.

Fluff made a face: she was not very fond of shopping. "What about telling Mr Jones that we've seen the bearded man again?"

"We'll do that on the way back."

"Perhaps I'll see Willybach again."

"Perhaps you will."

On their way into town Uncle Charles slowed up and pulled close into the side of the narrow road to give way to a red mini-car coming from the opposite direction. Leonie Bretherton was driving. She signalled her thanks to Uncle Charles and smiled as she passed.

"She may be a fibber, Uncle, but I still like her," Fluff declared firmly.

"H'm," replied the driver. And Fluff, looking at him, decided that he had gone 'all policemanlike', and she knew that it was best not to pursue the matter.

In fact Uncle Charles seemed preoccupied all through lunch, and Fluff went off round the shops wondering what was on his mind.

They had agreed to meet again at the car park. Fluff got there first, and spent the time waiting for her uncle by studying the queer mixture of people who came and went, and stood about in little groups gossiping in the bright sunlight.

The gossipers were mostly farming folk. The men were small and wiry, all rather like their own Mr Jones, and the women were tiny and neat with lively attractive faces.

Fluff wished she could understand what they were talking about, for her imagination was caught by the musical rise and fall of their native Welsh tongue, and the conversation was interspersed with sudden lilting laughter and much solemn shaking of heads. "I expect it's terribly difficult to learn to speak Welsh," she thought.

Just then Uncle Charles came up behind her and rested his hand on her shoulder. "One bright new penny for your thoughts," he offered.

As the car threaded its way through the busy streets, Fluff told her uncle of how she wished she could understand Welsh. "It seems such a jolly language, and yet it sounds at times as though the people are going to fight. They get so excited and then, quite suddenly, they are all smiles again."

"I believe it's a very beautiful language, Fluff, and when they sing it becomes even more lovely."

They drove on in silence for a while and then Uncle Charles asked, "Aren't you curious about my telephone call?"

Fluff turned to look at him.

"I've been talking to Scotland Yard," he said.

She was immediately interested. "About the fingerprint?"

"Yes, and other things."

"Was it made by Caradoc Evans?"

Uncle Charles shook his head. "No," he announced. And glimpsing Fluff's disappointed face, he quickly continued, "Much more interesting. The fingerprint on that brass does match one in Criminal Records, but it belongs to Buss Frisby!"

"Gosh!" said Fluff, flabbergasted. "Whatever does that mean?"

"It means, Fluff, that there must have been some link-up between Frisby and Evans during the past month."

"Frisby has been in Evans's shop?"

"I think he must have been."

"What happens now, Uncle?"

"Someone is coming down from Scotland Yard to make enquiries." A note of bitterness crept into his voice. "You see, Fluff, I'm not a policeman now."

Fluff could think of nothing to say which would help, but touched her uncle on the arm in a gesture of understanding.

As they approached the green gateway to Mr Jones's farm Uncle Charles said, "We'll call in and tell Mr Jones that the bearded man is still hanging about Caffryn-Mawr. It's time he mentioned it to the local police. Hop out and look after the gate while I drive through."

Fluff did not return to the car. A black and white dog came bounding towards her with a noisy welcome. "Willybach!" she called. And in a moment there was a tumbled mass of girl and dog rolling on the grass verge.

"Daft pair!" laughed Uncle Charles going up to the front door of the farmhouse, where both Mr and Mrs Jones had appeared in some haste to see what the noise was about.

"Let them get on with it," smiled Mr Jones. "They are both young, very young."

"Come you in," invited Mrs Jones, "and have a cup of tea. I've just made a fresh pot for our other visitor."

It was then that Uncle Charles noticed the small green delivery van in the farmyard. Boldly painted on boards fixed to the sides of the van were the words, *C. Evans – Antique Dealer, Dolgelley.*

"It is only Mr Evans from Dolgelley," explained Mrs Jones, as she led the way down the stone-flagged passage to the kitchen. "He is after persuading me to part with our old dresser, but I do not want to do that."

"Even though it's good money he's offering," put in Mr Jones.

The antique dealer rose from his chair when they entered the kitchen. "Why, if it isn't Mr Frost!" he cried. "What a surprise; although I did think that I saw you outside my shop the other day."

"Gracious me!" exclaimed Mrs Jones. "Fancy you two knowing each other. Whatever next!"

Uncle Charles merely remarked, "It's a surprisingly small world isn't it, Mr Evans, and time passes remarkably quickly?"

Evans nodded. "Sometimes, sometimes."

Mrs Jones poured out a cup of tea for the newcomer, and Uncle Charles stirred it thoughtfully for a moment.

"You'll not be holding the past against me, will you, Inspector?" queried Evans unexpectedly. And then he added, "Fair enough, I deserved everything I got and I served my sentence and paid up in full. When I got out I got a chance to go straight, and I don't want the past held against me forever."

His voice, no longer ingratiating, sounded as though he meant what he said, and Fluff, standing in the doorway with a now quiet Willybach, wanted to believe he was telling the truth.

Mr and Mrs Jones looked uncomfortable. But Mrs Jones ended the awkward silence by saying, "We take people here as we find them, Mr Frost, and since Mr Evans came he's been a good neighbour and a fair man to do business with."

Uncle Charles raised his eyebrows at the mention of neighbour, and Evans quickly explained, "When I came out of prison my uncle, who owned Caffryn-Mawr then, gave me a job on the farm. It was hard work but I was used to that; and when he died last year the old man left me the property."

He paused, and then continued. "I didn't know enough about running a farm to make it pay, and when Mr Jones here offered me a good price for the place, I was only too glad to take it. It gave me a chance to buy my little business in Dolgelley, and now I make a fair living . . . Almost honestly," he added, with a wry chuckle.

"What do you mean by *almost* honestly?" asked Uncle Charles, remembering only too well a certain fingerprint.

"Well, not all my brasses are genuine antiques although they're made in Wales: I've a little plant of my own for smelting and moulding. As for the wrought iron lamps and things, well those are mostly made by me during the winter months at my own forge. It's a trade I learned when I was in prison."

Again there was an awkward silence, and once more it was the sympathetic Mrs Jones who broke it. "They are very nice things which Mr Evans makes; much nicer than real antiques."

Uncle Charles, still very severe, said, "You realise everyone still thinks you know where the rest of the gold went to?" And looking him straight in the eye, he asked, "Do you?"

Evans shook his head. "No, Inspector, I don't. I said it in Court under oath, and I'll say it again now: I don't! All I know is what I told you at the time. Frisby and I split the load into two lots. Mine was left in a van in a car park at Barnet, and we went off to bury his share at his sister's place at Epping. You nabbed us there, and that's all I know."

"You also know," said Uncle Charles, "that when we took you out to Barnet to show us where you left the van, there was no van there."

"That's right, Inspector, it had gone. Someone had taken it."

"H'm, if it was ever there!"

Evans had shrunk into a pathetic little figure, and Fluff was beginning to feel sorry for him now.

He shrugged his shoulders dejectedly and hopelessly. "If I could tell you where it was Inspector, I would."

"Well, Evans, let's give you the benefit of the doubt. But I'm warning you, if you do ever touch that gold, you'll be letting yourself in for another sentence."

Evans shuddered. "Yes, Inspector, I know that." He

4

made to leave the room. "Come and see my little shop properly, and bring the little girl. There are one or two pretty things she'd like."

"All right, we'll come and see you tomorrow. And if your wrought iron work is good I'll buy something for my flat."

Once again Evans turned to go, and this time, in moving across the room, he reached out to run caressing fingers over the polished wood of the magnificent black oak dresser which took up almost one wall of the kitchen. "You are sure you won't change your mind, Mrs Jones?"

"No, Mr Evans, I just can't part with it. It belonged to my grandfather's father, and I won't let it go, not to you or anyone."

Evans smiled. "I shall try again," he said. "I shall try again."

A few minutes later they heard his van chugging off on the road back to Dolgelley.

"A strange encounter," remarked Uncle Charles.

"He's a strange man," replied Mrs Jones. "But I can only say, Mr Frost, what I said before: we take people here very much as we find them."

"Yes," agreed Mr Jones. "If he did wrong, he has paid for it. Now if the man wants to go straight, I'd just as soon help as hinder him."

So for a while the seemingly repentant Mr Evans was dismissed from their minds, and Uncle Charles raised the matter of the intruder at Caffryn-Mawr.

He asked first if Miss Bretherton had mentioned the incident of the morning when Fluff fell in the sheep-dip tank.

"Oh you poor mite," exclaimed Mrs Jones.

But Fluff only grinned and declared, "It's all right, really. Uncle Charles says I'm not good enough to die young."

Apparently Leonie Bretherton had not been back to the farm for lunch, and Mr Jones had been given no further news of the bearded man.

"I think it's something you ought to report to the police," insisted Uncle Charles. "From all accounts he's an unpleasant character, and you've quite a few things of value in the outbuildings, if not in the house itself."

"I think perhaps you are right, Mr Frost. I'll speak to the Sergeant at Dolgelley this evening."

Uncle Charles then turned the talk back to the subject of Leonie Bretherton.

There was no doubt that she was well liked at the farm. "Very quiet she is," said Mrs Jones, "and no trouble to us at all. We do not take many guests, but when she called here and said she wanted to do some paintings, we were pleased to let her a room."

"She has been with us a fortnight now, and two lovely pictures she has made," said Mr Jones. "Come and see," he invited.

He led the way to what was obviously a little-used drawing-room, from which emerged a smell of old damp and new turpentine as he opened the door.

There were two canvasses drying out on the newspaper-protected table. One was a picture of a bridge and a twisted tree. "That's by the old gold mine," explained Mrs Jones.

The other was a street scene of Dolgelley, with the antique shop in the foreground. "Mr Evans would like to buy that picture," said Mr Jones, "but Miss Bretherton is asking a lot of money for it. Twenty pounds, I believe."

"They are both very good," Uncle Charles said after he had looked closely into each of them. "The gold mine interests me quite a lot. Where is it exactly?"

"Just over the other side of Dolgelley. It hasn't been used for years and years and years."

Fluff joined in, "It would look lovely over our mantelpiece, Uncle, honestly it would."

"But, Fluff, I can't afford twenty pounds, just like that, for pictures now that I've retired."

"But that one, Mr Frost, is only eight guineas."

The voice of Leonie Bretherton from the doorway startled them all.

"Oh, Uncle," cried Fluff anxiously, "you must buy it now, you really must!"

"That's a big difference, Miss Bretherton," remarked Uncle Charles. "A very strange difference."

"Not at all, Mr Frost, not at all. I sell my paintings to whom I please, at the price which pleases me. To you my price is eight guineas."

"Done," said Uncle Charles, and felt for his wallet.

"No, leave the money until you pick up the picture. It will be much easier to handle when you leave, and dry enough to travel undamaged. Besides, where could you keep it in a caravan?"

"How have you been getting on today, my dear?" asked Mrs Jones, when they had returned to the kitchen.

"Not too badly, after a poor start. In fact the picture is almost finished. Would you like to see it?"

She disappeared from the room without waiting for

an answer, and went to her car. She was quickly back again.

With the painting held up for them to study, Fluff could see that it had developed quite noticeably from the state it had been in when she had last seen it. Now, included in the middle distance were a man, three dogs and some sheep.

"Gosh!" exclaimed Fluff. "Isn't that Mr Jones with Willybach and the other dogs?"

Leonie nodded.

Mrs Jones enquired, "May we buy this one, Miss Bretherton? We really would love to have it."

Leonie Bretherton laughed. "This looks like being a profitable holiday. We'll do a deal on it shall we?" She paused. "I'll exchange it for two weeks accommodation. But first, I'd like to exhibit it in London. I'm rather proud of it."

A little later Fluff and her uncle said their goodbyes and, with a special hug for Willybach from Fluff, they set off for their caravan home.

"I do like Miss Bretherton," insisted Fluff, "even if she does tell fibs about burnt umber."

But back at the caravan more doubts began to arise. There were signs of disturbance, as though someone had made a thorough search for something.

Uncle Charles examined the lock on the door with a professional eye. "It's one which could be picked quite easily with a hair grip and a little bit of skill and patience."

And, at that point, John returned from his climb, and confirmed their worst suspicions. "One of the chaps lent me a jolly good pair of field glasses when we were coming down. I took a look at the caravan to see if you were about, but all I saw was that artist woman. She was coming out of the door."

Chapter Six

Uncle Charles in Harness Again

Early the next morning, in fact so early that breakfast was still in progress, a small sports car drew up by the caravan. Its driver, a tall solemn young man, who called Uncle Charles "Sir", was introduced to John and Fluff as Sergeant Southgate. With him came a long, official envelope, and from it he produced a personal note in the Assistant Commissioner's handwriting. This was opened with care by Uncle Charles. He read it with considerable interest, and much pleasure.

"You know what's in this letter, Sergeant?"

"Yes Sir, I do. And personally, I hope you'll see your way clear to accepting the A.C.'s invitation to take charge of the enquiries down here."

"I would certainly like to. As far as I'm concerned, I've always felt this Frisby-Evans business was an unsatisfactory affair, with half the gold still to be found. Now that Frisby has escaped we are almost back to where we started seven years ago."

Sergeant Southgate dug his hand into the envelope again, and this time he brought out a special warrant card, which he handed to the older man with a respectful smile. "You'll need this then," he said. "It only requires your signature, Sir, to make it effective!"

"The A.C. was as sure as that, was he? The sly old dog!"

With the card duly signed and safely pocketed, Uncle Charles helped clear the table. "Now, you two, you can get on with the washing up while I put Sergeant Southgate fully in the picture." There he paused, in mock seriousness, to warn Fluff, "as for you, young woman, one word of interruption, and I'll have the Sergeant handcuff you to a tree well out of earshot. So watch it, Miss!"

Fluff grinned and retorted, "Dear Uncle, and Inspector, Sir, my lips are sealed."

So while John washed and Fluff dried, Uncle Charles related recent developments.

Sergeant Southgate made no comment but jotted down one or two points in his notebook.

Then came the summing up. "So you see, we now have an Evans who is making out, in a most convincing and heart-breaking manner, that he is going straight and hasn't any knowledge of the gold; and yet, at the same time, there's this curious fingerprint link with Frisby, who is on the run."

Uncle Charles paused and lit his pipe. "We also have an extraordinary young woman behaving in a most peculiar manner, and taking far too great an interest in the farm, Evans and us. And finally, there's this bearded man hanging around."

Sergeant Southgate put down his notebook. "And you think that could be Frisby, hiding out in the farm-house with Evans's knowledge and help?"

"My mind has been running that way. What's the latest news from the Yard on the Frisby hunt? I know the newspapers gave out an account, about a week ago, that he was believed to be in Ireland."

"The Dublin police are still checking. The story came in from a good source, so they say, and his sister at Epping has had a letter from him with a Dublin post-mark."

"How do you know that?"

"We've been making enquiries there, and she showed us the letter."

Uncle Charles rubbed his chin thoughtfully. "What did it say?"

"It was very brief. It merely said he was safe with friends, and would let her know later how to contact him. There was no address, of course."

"Did you check the writing?"

"Yes, it's Frisby's all right."

"I'm still doubtful. It's far too easy a trick to pull in these days of fast planes. Someone could have posted it for him – even that sister of his. She's a hard nut with no love for the police, and I wouldn't trust her any more than I trust that precious brother of hers. He could be anywhere; here for instance."

Uncle Charles rubbed his chin again in thought. "What photographs have you brought with you?" he asked.

This time the envelope yielded two packets of prints.

Fluff, making an excuse to lean across the table while she put some crockery away on a shelf, sneaked a quick look. One set of photographs was of Evans, but an Evans in many ways different to the man in the shop.

The other photographs had been turned face downwards, except one which was partly concealed by Uncle Charles's hand. This he was working on with a pencil.

He looked up to smile at her. "You can look in a moment, Miss! This is being done for your benefit anyway. You are the only one of us to have got a glimpse of the bearded man's face. Now look."

Fluff took the print and John, wiping his hands, moved up to look over her shoulder. It was an unpleasant face, with close-set eyes which peered up from the picture. The pencilled beard did little to hide the vicious mouth.

"Is it him?"

Fluff nodded. "Yes, I'm sure it is."

Sergeant Southgate asked, "Now what?"

"Can't we hunt him out?" exclaimed John.

"No, John," replied Uncle Charles. "That's the last thing we want to do for the moment. We might be lucky and catch him in the house, if that's where he is hiding, but I think if we were to do that, we might well lose our best chance of getting a lead on the missing gold. We'll alert the local police and get a watch put on the area, but we don't want to alarm either man yet."

Sergeant Southgate put in, "You think, Sir, that the gold might be hereabouts?"

"It's just possible. Evans and Frisby got away with the shipment on New Year's Day, but it was two days before we picked them up in Epping. There would have been time for them to have got here, disposed of it, and got back to London."

"That's probably why Evans made his way back here as soon as he could after his sentence was over."

Fluff was almost bursting with excitement. She exploded, "Then all that gold might be hidden here, and we might find it!"

"Steady, Fluff, steady, just take it easy," Uncle Charles said dampeningly. "Don't get too excited. Evans is a shrewd bird and he's had plenty of opportunity to dispose of a lot of it. Besides, we can't be sure it was here in the first place. It's all a good deal of guess work. Both he and Frisby stuck persistently to the story that they had lost the van containing the other half of the shipment."

"I bet they *didn't* lose it!" said John. "And what's more, I bet I know where the gold is at this very moment!"

They all looked at him, Fluff in astonishment, and Uncle Charles and Sergeant Southgate in amused disbelief.

"All right," announced John, holding the floor, "isn't there a saying that all that glitters isn't gold?"

Uncle Charles corrected him: "All that glisters . . . "

John grinned. "O.K., all that glisters then . . . but," and here he paused dramatically, "all that shines needn't be brass!"

Fluff cried, "You mean that it's staring everyone in the face in the antique shop?"

"That's quite an idea, John," said his uncle. "It's the sort of idea, too, that would appeal to a clever bird like Evans. You could quite easily hide half a ton of gold right under everyone's nose like that, and keep an eye on it yourself without any difficulty!"

"What about people wanting to buy bits of it?" asked the Sergeant, but then answered his own question. "I suppose he could stick little labels on the gold objects saying they were sold, or say they were flawed and offer a duplicate piece in real brass."

"H'm!" said Uncle Charles. "It's certainly an idea worth looking into. I think Fluff, John and I will take up Mr Evans's kind invitation to take a look round his shop. If there are any pieces he seems reluctant to part with, it might be worth examining them with a great deal of care."

Back in harness again as Chief Detective Inspector Frost, he began issuing his orders quietly, briskly and efficiently. Sergeant Southgate was to liaise with the local police and ask them to put an unobtrusive net round the farm, and he was to inform Scotland Yard of his actions. The Chief Inspector added, "While you are on to the Yard you'd better make some enquiries about Miss Leonie Bretherton."

"Any leads?"

Uncle Charles gave him a brief, but very graphic description, and her car number. Fluff wondered at his memory for detail as the Sergeant made notes in his book.

'That should be enough to work on, Sir."

Arrangements were made for a meeting later that day at the hotel where Sergeant Southgate was staying, and a few minutes later after John had accompanied him to the gate to let his car through, he was on his way.

Fluff, putting a comb through her hair, said, "Uncle Charles . . . "

"Yes."

"I do hope Miss Bretherton isn't mixed up in this. I do like her."

"We'll have to wait and see, Fluff. But why this sudden solicitude?"

Fluff wasn't quite sure what solicitude meant, but she said solemnly, "Well, I just think she is nice." Then she added, "And if you send her to prison she won't be able to paint pictures."

"Well, Fluff, between you and me I think she's rather nice too, so I also hope it won't come to prison for her."

No more was said on the subject, and before long the three of them were on their way to a certain antique shop in Dolgelley.

Chapter Seven

The Unhappy Mr Evans

It had not been a good morning for the dealer in Welsh antiques.

The first ring of the shop bell, just after nine o'clock, was not for a customer, but for Buss Frisby's sister.

Like a figure of doom she stood silently by the counter. Her eyes, close-set like her brother's, held no warmth of greeting as Evans pushed aside the curtain which screened the living quarters from the shop.

"I told you to keep away from here," he said angrily. "You'll bring the cops in on us if they see us together."

"I've not been followed."

"What do you want?"

"You know what I want, and you know what Buss wants. We want our fair share. Split three ways."

"You can have it but you'll have to wait."

"I'm sick and tired of waiting, and so is Buss. I saw him the other night . . ."

"Where? Up at the farm?"

"No, at the cottage where we get the signal from the road."

"You fools!"

"What do you mean?"

"Did you see a caravan?"

"Yes – I kept well clear of it."

"Do you know who's staying in it?"

"Buss says he's seen a couple of kids hanging around, and there's a man with them."

"A man! It's that rotten Frost from the Yard. Of all the bad luck!"

The woman was suddenly whitefaced. "Do you think he knows anything?"

"He knows I'm here, and if he as much as catches a glimpse of Buss he'll know something else is in the wind. Frost is no fool."

"Well, we'd better get Buss out quickly. But he won't get far without money." She looked at Evans fiercely. "We just can't wait, so you'd better cough up right away."

Evans wrung his hands desperately. "You know what I told you both the other night. It isn't easy. If I put too much out at any one time, somebody will smell a rat."

"How much are you going to get for the stuff that's out now?"

"Twenty thousand, if we're lucky."

"That'll do for the moment. It will get Buss out of the country."

Evans asked, "How?"

"I've got a ship fixed at Cardiff for eight days' time. It's costing eight hundred pounds to fix a passage to Buenos Aires, and payment has to be made in advance."

Evans whistled through his teeth. "The money will be here on Friday; used one pound notes and American dollars."

The woman was looking at him thoughtfully. "If Frost is up at that farm, we must get Buss out of the house. What about hiding him down here again?"

"Too dangerous! One night was enough. You know I caught him looking at stuff in the shop?"

"He's curious! He wants to know where you've stowed it away."

Evans grimaced. He knew what she meant. "It's somewhere where neither he, you, nor anybody else will find it in a hurry. I'm not telling *anyone*."

Her smile was evil. "If Buss wants to he'll find out. He'll make you talk. He's got ways."

Evans's mouth was set in a grim line. "We'll see about that. In the meantime, he's got to get out of that farmhouse and further up the hill before Frost sees him. A shepherd's hut will do."

"You'd best get him extra blankets then. He's running out of food too, and cigarettes."

"All right, I'll see him tonight. He'll be looking out for a signal at the usual times?"

"Yes," she said. "He'll be waiting at the old cottage. You'd best watch him. He's had about enough of being out there cooped up on his own. Tell him he'll be picked up on Saturday when I've got the money."

"Where are you going now?"

"Back to Barmouth. Give me a ring at my hotel if I'm wanted. You know my number."

He watched her depart, hate glittering in his eyes. Then he lit a cigarette with shaking fingers, and muttered to himself, "Split three ways? That's what *she* thinks!"

It was about an hour later when Uncle Charles arrived at the shop with John and Fluff.

Evans was busy with a man and his overfat wife who, from their accents, were American.

"Why, Elmer, isn't this just too cute?"

Elmer grunted noncommittally, as he gave a brief look at the twisted brass door-knocker with the impish face which so pleased his lady.

Evans's voice was deferential as he brought other pieces out for them to see and then, for a moment, he left the counter to speak to the three newcomers.

"Just have a look round while you are waiting, Mr Frost, and then, when I'm free, I'll take you over to my workshop. There are one or two pieces of ironwork I'm specially proud of which I'd like you to look at."

It was a surprisingly big and well laid out shop. Evans had obviously given a lot of thought to the best way to display his stock.

At some time the floor of the room above had been removed. A gallery now ran round the walls, railed in exquisitely fashioned wrought iron. In this was set a series of panels cast in the shape of ladies wearing old Welsh costume with tall steeple hats. The winding stairways to the gallery were railed in a similar manner, and the same picturesque motif was used in the four alcoves, which were subtly lit by concealed lights. The few pieces of antique furniture and china on display were first class examples of Welsh workmanship, but what mostly caught the eye was the gleaming brassware. This filled shelf upon shelf both on the ground floor and in the gallery.

"Phew!" whispered John, "Have we got to examine this lot?"

Uncle Charles was picking up pieces at random but looking closely at each, weighing them in his hands and discreetly using his thumbnail to test the surface.

He shook his head. "It's not a job for us, John. It would need someone more expert to be sure. Most things are lacquered, and their appearance gives nothing away. Don't look so disappointed, Fluff," he added, "or you will give our game away."

The two Americans completed their purchases, and made arrangements for them to be packed and sent to their home in Washington.

"It's amazing how much of my stuff goes abroad," said Evans, as he joined Uncle Charles and the youngsters. "Americans in particular seem to be great collectors. But you know, I never tell them it is antique unless it is. I say it's genuine Welsh manufacture, which is true. Let me show you."

He led them through the curtained doorway, across a neatly furnished living-room, to a building in the yard beyond. This was fitted out as a workshop. He was obviously very proud of it.

"What's this?" asked an immensely interested John.

"That's a small electric furnace for smelting the brass. It comes in those ingots that you can see in the corner."

Uncle Charles picked up an ingot from the small pile. "Does brass weigh less than gold?" he asked.

Evans reproved him with a smile and a chuckle, which did not ring quite true. "Now, Inspector, that was not a nice question to ask me at all, now was it?"

Fluff was closely examining one of the moulds into which the molten brass was poured. "That's for a Welsh dragon which holds a matchbox," explained Evans. He produced a dull-looking casting from a rack. "It comes out from the mould like this, and then I put a polish on it with a buffing wheel."

He pressed a switch, and a cloth wheel, thick with green polish, began to revolve rapidly and noisily. Working the surface of the brass against the edge of this wheel he quickly obtained an all-over polish to the casting.

"Would you like it, young lady?"

Fluff nodded. "Yes please, Mr Evans."

"Well, if you want it to stay shiny and bright, without the bother of polishing it every day, give it a coat of lacquer. Use this brush."

Fluff busied herself with her matchbox dragon, and Evans took Uncle Charles and John across to his forge. On the racks were pieces of wrought ironwork in varying stages of completion, and strips of bar iron lying ready for working.

The forge was cold. "This is a job for the winter months," explained Evans. "There's no point in keeping the shop open then, and I can get on with building up my stock for the tourist season."

"It looks as though you've got a nice little business here Mr Evans."

"I have, Inspector, I have. It's a very nice little business. You'd really be surprised if you knew how much my stock and shop was worth."

There was a look almost of challenge in the antique dealer's face, but Uncle Charles refused to rise to the bait. He had a feeling that secretly the man was laughing at him.

"Well, Mr Evans, it's all very interesting. What I would like to look at is one of those wrought iron table lamps in your shop; and if my niece has finished painting her dragon . . . "

Fluff looked up. "Yes, it's finished, but it's not dry."

"Leave it here, young lady," said Evans. "You'll be in Dolgelley again another day, and you can pick it up then."

He led the way back to the shop, and Uncle Charles indicated the lamp which interested him. "How much, Mr Evans? This one isn't ticketed. I hope it's for sale?"

"Everything on these shelves is for sale, Inspector." Again there was a not completely concealed note of mockery in the voice. "The lamp, to you . . . Let me see – shall we say three pounds fifty?"

Uncle Charles, inwardly seething, nodded acceptance and took out his wallet.

"Wait a minute! I've put some other things aside for you to see."

"Not today, Mr Evans. I'll have a look at those when we come in to pick up the brass dragon, if you don't mind." With this, he handed over the money and picked up the lamp.

"As you like, Inspector, as you like. You know you are always welcome."

He ushered them from the shop still smiling; but the smile disappeared as he turned from the street and remembered his earlier visitor, and the task that lay before him that evening.

Chapter Eight

Dog Talk

It was a frustrated Chief Inspector Frost who arrived at the Jones's farm to find that Leonie Bretherton was out, and wouldn't be back until the following afternoon.

"It was to London she said she was going," Mrs Jones replied in answer to his question. "And she will have to stay overnight."

"Confound it!" exploded Uncle Charles. "I particularly wanted to talk to that young woman."

"But she left you a message, Mr Frost, just in case you called. I will go and get it for you. No, better still, you must come in and sit down in comfort to read it."

She led the way through to the kitchen and reached for an envelope on the mantelpiece.

It contained a single sheet of notepaper and two pieces of wire, each holding a small lead seal. The message was short: *These should mean something to you. One I found near the burial chamber on the hill; the other was among the ashes in the outhouse at the farm.*

"Do they mean anything?" asked Fluff.

Uncle Charles held out the seals so that they could both see the stamped E.A.B. "That stands for European and Asian Bank. The cases which contained the bullion were all secured by wire and sealed in this way."

"Then the gold must have been on the farm, Uncle?"

"Yes, John, it looks very much like it."

"Oh, that dreadful Mr Evans, to tell such downright wicked lies, and in this very room too!"

"What's all this, Gwynneth?" enquired Mr Jones from the doorway. "You must not upset yourself so."

Everyone, except Fluff, who was much too involved with Willybach, tried to tell him all about it at the same time. And with Willybach giving a noisy greeting to his favourite friend there was, for a moment, pandemonium in the kitchen.

"Good gracious me!" cried Mr Jones. "One at a time please! As for you Willybach . . . " He gave some short sharp commands in Welsh which quietened the dog, and made him sit obediently on the hearthrug. "Now perhaps someone will explain."

Uncle Charles gave what explanation there was, but Mr Jones was still looking puzzled. "But why should Miss Bretherton leave you such a note Mr Frost?"

"That I don't know, but I expect we shall have an answer to that question when she gets back from London."

Mrs Jones insisted upon Uncle Charles and the children staying to lunch. "It's no bother. There's my own home-cured bacon in the larder . . . " – she opened the larder door to show the huge side of bacon hanging from the hook in the ceiling – "and you'll not have tasted the like of it for years, Mr Frost. There are peas and potatoes from the garden, and we'll finish up with a blackcurrant jam tart with the top off the morning's milk."

John and Fluff helped Mr Jones to pick extra peas and to dig two roots of potatoes, and before long, they were sitting down to a meal of real country fare, the kind of meal that can't be bettered anywhere in the world.

"And no Oriental *thank you's* afterwards," whispered Fluff to John.

During lunch the talk turned from Evans and the gold to dogs. This was because the much privileged Willybach was allowed to remain in the house, whereas the other dogs, not such friendly creatures, lived outside. Willybach was sitting close to Fluff's chair hoping for scraps. His tail made a steady thump, thump, on the floor.

"Does Willybach understand English?" asked Fluff.

Mr Jones, in mock seriousness, spoke to the dog in Welsh, and Mrs Jones bubbled with laughter. "You must not tease."

"What did you say?" asked Fluff.

"I asked Willybach if he spoke English. Didn't you see him shake his head, and hear him say no?"

There was a merry twinkle in Mr Jones's deep blue eyes. Willybach's head was to one side with his ears cocked. He had a puzzled, worried expression, but settled down again when Mr Jones used a softly spoken, almost caressing phrase, again in Welsh.

"After lunch you must teach Fiona how to talk to Willybach," suggested Mrs Jones to her husband. "She will learn quickly for she is young and her voice has not yet set."

So it was that, after the meal, Mr Jones took Fluff and Willybach out to a paddock at the back of the farm, and, much amused, Uncle Charles and John leant over a gate to watch the first lesson in Welsh.

"Now," said Mr Jones, "to get him to lie down you say GORWEDD!" Willybach lay down obediently.

"To go forward – YMALN!" Again Willybach obeyed, and moved forward a few paces.

"You try this time Fiona. Remember GORWEDD is 'lie down', and YMALN is 'forward'."

To Fluff, *gorwedd* sounded like 'gorweth' and *ymaln* like 'd'larn'. She tried both, hesitantly.

Willybach, not quite sure, hesitated himself, but trying to be helpful repeated his former movements, first lying down and then getting up and moving forward. He looked round at his audience, his gentle brown eyes plainly asking, "Did I do the right thing?"

"Bravo!" called Uncle Charles.

"Jolly good!" echoed John.

"Now let's try again. Listen, GORWEDD, and then YMALN!" This time Willybach was much more sure.

Mr Jones called, "'DYRI YMA!" The dog came to him at once, and was rewarded with a pat and a biscuit.

Whilst Willybach was busy crunching this with his strong white teeth, Mr Jones moved Fluff about ten yards away from the dog and gave her another biscuit in readiness.

"You try. Remember? For 'come here', you say DYRI YMA!"

Fluff tried: "Derra ma!" Willybach had no doubts about this and sprang towards her for the biscuit.

"*Gam bullch!*" cried Mr Jones, interpreting straight away, "steady, steady."

"Gambulch!" repeated Fluff.

Willybach steadied, and, so it seemed, smiled quite happily as he got busy with his second biscuit.

"That's very good," said Mr Jones, patting Fluff on the shoulder. "Either Willybach's behaving himself today, or else you've got more influence over the rascal than I have."

"*Dyri yma!*" called Fluff gleefully, and, catching Willybach in her arms as he leapt towards her, they both rolled around on the grass with the dog pulling gently at her jersey.

When they got back to the house Mr Jones put the commands down on a slip of paper, and wrote against each call an indication of the pronunciation.

Fluff practised all the way to the caravan. She was thrilled by what she had overheard Mr Jones saying to her uncle. "You know, Mr Frost, it's a great gift indeed to be able to handle animals and understand them. My old grandfather had the gift; he could have the very birds feeding from his hand. And he was a real wonder with dogs. He even seemed to be able to talk to them in their own language. Young Fiona there, seems to be blessed in the same way. Animals know they can trust her."

Fluff's reverie was interrupted on arrival at the caravan, when John, with his mind more on gold than dogs, asked, "What happens next, Uncle?"

"For the moment, nothing, John. We'll just have to wait until we hear how Sergeant Southgate got on today. But we'll probably not be able to do much until Miss Bretherton comes back."

"Then I vote we go for a swim," said Fluff.

So swimming they went.

At six o'clock that evening, as previously arranged, they met Sergeant Southgate in a quiet corner of the residents' lounge of his hotel.

His report was brief. The local police would be putting a watch on the roads, and the railway and bus stations. The farmhouse and Evans would also be kept under observation.

"What about Miss Bretherton?" asked Uncle Charles.

Here Sergeant Southgate had drawn almost a complete blank. The car, purchased six months previously, was registered in her name; and her address, according to the licensing particulars, was a self-contained flat in West Hampstead, London.

"I've got someone checking for more details, but we shan't get a report until tomorrow, Sir."

"Is there any news from Dublin?"

"Nothing definite. The Irish police still think the tip they had was a good one, and not a plant, but there have been no more letters. Of course, Frisby's sister is away at the moment."

"Does anyone know where?"

"The neighbour who is looking after her cat says she's on holiday. At Cardiff, she thinks."

Uncle Charles was silent for a moment. "The sister's movements are worth looking into. I'm certain she was behind the scenes at the time of the robbery, but we couldn't pin anything on her. She was away from home at the time we picked up Frisby and Evans, and she produced an alibi we couldn't shake."

"You know, Sir, I am sure she must have been mixed up in Frisby's Dartmoor break. He could never have got away from the 'Moor' without help of some kind."

"Right, Sergeant. Get the Cardiff police moving and see what they can find out. You haven't got a picture of her I suppose?"

"No, only a description, but I'll get on to Epping as well as Cardiff, and see what can be done."

Sergeant Southgate busied himself with his notebook for a moment. "What about you, Sir?" he asked, looking up. "How have you got on?"

"How indeed!" rumbled Uncle Charles. "We've had a most frustrating day."

He then told of the fruitless visit to Evans's shop, and of the disappearance of Leonie Bretherton. "We did get *these* of course."

Sergeant Southgate examined the seals with interest. "Is it worth pulling Evans in for questioning?"

"Not yet. We'll see what tomorrow brings forth when we've had a chance to talk to the Bretherton woman."

That night as Fluff snuggled down between the sheets at bedtime, her thoughts were far away from gold,

Evans and Frisby. To her the day had brought a closer understanding of her new and deeply loved friend.

"*Dyri yma,*" she murmured, sleepily and happily.

Chapter Nine

Nothing to Report

It was Sergeant Southgate who unwittingly allowed Evans to carry out his mission that night, unhampered and unobserved.

Just after ten o'clock, he and the Station Sergeant were sitting together in the Police Station, discussing some local aspects of the bullion case, when the telephone rang.

The Constable who was keeping a discreet eye on the antique dealer's shop was calling to say that, a few minutes before, Evans had appeared at an upstairs window wearing his pyjamas, and it looked as though he was preparing for bed. "And his light's just gone out, Sergeant. I can see the window from this call box."

"Hold on a minute, Hughes."

The Station Sergeant repeated the report to the C.I.D. man.

Southgate asked, "Do you want to pull your man off watch then?"

"If I can. We are shorthanded tonight, with the special checks on the main roads, and I want someone for the patrol up at Colwyn Quarry. We've been keeping a man on duty there at night, because the explosives store was broken into about a fortnight ago, and a whole box of gelignite and a packet of detonators were stolen."

"O.K., bring him in. But make sure that someone is on the Evans job before six o'clock. He might be an early riser."

The Station Sergeant spoke into the telephone. "Right, Hughes. Come back to the station. You can take your bike and do the quarry patrol."

So at eleven o'clock, when the wily Evans took a cautious look up and down the street from a window in the gallery next to his bedroom, there was no watcher in sight.

He dressed quickly in the dark, smiling to himself at his own cleverness. "If old Foxy Frost thinks I haven't spotted what he's up to, he's got another think coming. Fancy putting Fatty Hughes on to watch the place. He sticks out a mile!"

But Evans did not relax his vigilance as he crept out through the back way of the house and made his way up the dark and narrow side streets to the shed, on the outskirts of the town, where he kept his van.

He approached the shed cautiously, making sure there was no one around. Satisfied of this, he unlocked and opened the doors carefully. Then he pushed the van out on to the road, and, without starting the engine allowed it to roll gently forward.

"So far, so good," he muttered to himself, as he closed and locked the shed.

Quickly, he checked that the heavy rucksack he had packed and put into the van earlier in the day was still there and intact. Then he tested the torch that he kept in the pocket of the van door. There was something else in the same pocket, and this he took out, and transferred to his own jacket pocket. It was heavy and made an ugly bulge in the cloth. In the moment it had been exposed to the faint moonlight, a dull gleam showed on the blued steel of the squat barrel. He patted his pocket and grinned. A revolver was a comfortable thing to have handy when you were dealing with rats, particularly when you were dealing with vicious rats like Frisby.

Evans got into the van and, having released the brake, allowed it to coast gently down the road. When it had gathered sufficient speed he turned the ignition key, depressed the clutch and engaged gear. As he released the clutch, the engine coughed and came to life in readiness for the climb out of the town towards Caffryn Mawr. No one in the cottages near the garage heard a thing.

Once clear of the town, Evans switched on his headlights and began to hum a little tune to himself as he motored along. Things weren't so bad after all. He had made up his mind about what he was going to do and how he was going to do it. If all continued to go well, he would have no more bother from either Frisby or his sister – ever again.

His humming ceased when the van was still some distance from the gateway to Caffryn Mawr. He pulled off the road and on to the grass verge before switching off the lights and the engine. For a full minute he waited in the darkness, listening carefully before he stepped out of the van. He took with him the pack and the torch, and then made for a point on the roadside where he knew he could pick up signals from the cottage by the Druid's Stones.

A glance at the luminous dial on his watch told him he had twenty minutes to wait until midnight; twenty minutes to wait, twenty minutes to go over the plan in his mind, twenty minutes to make sure there were no snags in his plan. There must not be one single mistake.

The stars above him were bright, clear and hard. To the south, the black mass of the Cader Idris Mountains blocked out the lower sky. To the north, the Valley of the Mawddach fell away in a velvety darkness, which was broken once in a while by the lights of a car passing along the distant main road to Barmouth.

The tinkling sound of water running over stones, and the faraway roar of a waterfall only seemed to make the silence of the midnight hour more complete.

Evans looked up at the stars. These were the same stars he had stared at so often through the window of his prison cell. He had spent the longest part of his sentence in a cell where the window had been open to the northern sky, and through the criss-cross of iron bars, he had been able to trace how the widely flung constellation of the Plough had wheeled around on the axis of the Pole Star. The North Star had been a prisoner in one place in the sky just as he, himself, was imprisoned.

Evans turned to the north, and found that star again. He shivered, but the cause was not the coolness of the gentle night wind. It was the memory of those bleak nights and long days of prison life. He *would* not allow himself to be caught again.

Silently he cursed the man on the hill whose folly had caused their earlier downfall, and whose greed and viciousness might well lead to a second disaster. There was only one way to save himself, and he would follow it, determinedly, and without any scruple or regret. The sooner he could get rid of Frisby and his precious sister the better.

Stirring out of his reverie, Evans noticed the time, and flashed his light quickly, four times in succession. Four answering flashes came from the hill. Then two more flashes given from the hill signified that all was clear, and it was quite safe to approach the hut.

Evans's choice of route was much longer than that used by Frisby's sister two nights earlier. It was a route which took him well out of earshot of the caravan, and meant hard and difficult climbing as the pack was heavy.

At the hut Frisby was fuming. His greeting was curt as the little antique dealer appeared in the doorway.

"Took your time, didn't you?"

Evans unslung the pack before replying, "I had to give that caravan a wide berth."

"Got any fags?" Frisby was fumbling with the straps of the pack. "I ain't had one for hours."

"Don't open that up now; I've got some in my pocket."

A match glowed in the darkness between Frisby's cupped hands, and there was a momentary easing of tension as he drew in the first mouthful of smoke.

Evans used his torch to find a slab of stone on which to sit. "You know who's in the caravan, don't you?"

"Yep. Frost. I 'phoned Lil tonight, and she wised me up on that score."

"You fool! You'll get us all trapped again. Where did you phone from?"

"There's a call box about a mile down the road.

Nobody saw me. I had to know what was up."

"Frost is on to me. He was nosing about the shop today with two kids."

"He didn't find anything, I suppose, or you wouldn't be here," sneered Frisby.

"No, he didn't. Nobody could; not even Mr Clever Frost. He thought what you thought, and started looking through a whole lot of brass."

Sudden anger seemed to stir Frisby. "Well, where *have* you got it, you double-crossing little perisher? You needn't think twenty thousand pounds is enough to buy me off. I want a lot more than that, and so does Lil."

The butt of the revolver which he was holding in his pocket, gave a comforting feeling of courage to Evans.

He spoke sharply. "You'll get more. Both of you will get more, but only when I say so. You mucked things up before by talking too much in a pub, and I'm not taking any more chances. I've got it where neither you nor Frost can find it; and if you leave it to me to handle, we can all live in comfort for the rest of our lives."

Frisby moved quickly in the darkness but Evans was even quicker. "Stop being a fool, Buss! I've got a gun here and I'm quite ready to use it."

"You dirty little skunk!"

"Maybe. Now sit down, and I'll try and get a bit of sense into your thick skull."

Frisby sat down. He was breathing heavily with suppressed anger.

Evans went on, "Leave it to me, and I'll get rid of the gold bit by bit. That way no awkward questions will be asked, and I can get a good price for it. You'll get your share, and so will Lil, but you'll both have to trust me."

"Trust you? I wouldn't trust you any further than I could throw you."

The starlight from the doorway gleamed for a moment on the weapon in Evans's hand as he waved it before Frisby's angry eyes. "You'll have to, Buss. You've got no choice. Now listen to me. Tomorrow morning you'll move out of the farmhouse and go further up the mountain. Find a shepherd's hut, and stay out of sight. There's food and plenty of cigarettes in the pack, enough for four days, and a bottle of whisky to keep out the cold. Keep clear of Frost. If he as much as suspects you're here, he'll clamp down on me, and we'll never be able to pick up the money and get you away."

Frisby growled, "O.K., but don't make any mistakes. Gun or no gun, if you let me down on Saturday, I'll get you."

The threat only made Evans more determined than ever to follow through his plan to the end. Now was the time to let it appear that he was beginning to crack under the menaces.

"All right, I heard you. You'll get your money on Saturday; and the sooner you get it, and get off to South America, the better it'll be for all of us. There are times when I wished I'd never touched the job. The gold's been nothing but a curse."

Frisby gave a throaty chuckle. "If that's the way you feel about it, Doc, you'd better hand it all over to me. I ain't afraid of that kind of curse."

The antique dealer mumbled a reply which might have meant anything. The use of the old familiar "Doc", short for Caradoc, meant that Frisby had swallowed the bait!

In a more friendly mood they talked over the plans for the getaway. As Evans knew Frost had got an eye on him, it would have to be Lil who brought Frisby the money and the car for the journey to Cardiff.

"She'd better bring those two nuns' outfits as well," suggested Evans. "If Foxy Frost is watching me, he might have got people checking the main roads in case I make a break for it with the gold. It would be a fine catch if he picked *you* up. I think it would please him as much as getting the gold!"

Frisby swore, but laughed at the same time. He remembered with glee the way he and Lil had got through the patrols on Dartmoor, dressed up as two Sisters from the Tavistock Priory. Lil had been most convincing with her story of the Priory car, and the bundles of cast-off clothing for the "poor African people" which were on the back seat. Contained in one of these bundles was a suit of prison grey. The car, the nuns' habits, and the bundles of old clothing were now safely garaged in Barmouth. They could all play their part again.

"I'll phone Lil in the morning," said Evans, "and we can fix up the final details."

"Right, Doc."

With that, Evans departed and made his careful way back to the van.

He was humming quietly again as the van coasted silently down the hill into Dolgelley. All was going well. Soon he would be free of Buss Frisby and all his worries, including Foxy Frost. With Lil and Buss both out of the way for good where nobody would ever find them, Frost would not be able to get evidence from anyone; and he, Caradoc Evans, would be free, really free, at last!

By two o'clock Evans was safely back in bed. He slept better that night than he had slept since he had heard of Frisby's escape.

The constable who came on early morning duty could see nothing amiss. He telephoned to his Station Sergeant. "There's nothing to report, Sergeant."

Chapter Ten

In Which the Fox's Earth is Stopped

The starlit night was followed by a brilliant sunrise full of the promise of a really hot day.

"This," said Fluff at breakfast, "is just the day for another dip."

"H'm," said her uncle who had been thoughtfully silent all through the meal. "H'm."

"Oh, Uncle!" wailed Fluff. "Does your 'H'm' mean 'Yes', or does it mean 'No', or does it just mean that your thoughts are very much elsewhere?"

"Stop badgering, Fluff," put in John, "and pass the marmalade."

"Please . . . !"

"All right, Miss Particular. PASS THE MARMALADE, PLEASE!"

"Who said something about bathing today?" their Uncle suddenly asked.

"I did," answered Fluff.

"And I think it's a good idea too," added her brother. "It's going to be jolly hot. Phew! It's hot already."

"Fair enough, bathing it shall be – that is, providing Sergeant Southgate doesn't turn up with anything that requires immediate attention."

But ten minutes later, when the Sergeant arrived, they could tell at once that something big was in the wind.

"Things are beginning to break for us, Sir," he announced eagerly. "The Cardiff police have been on the phone this morning with a story that Frisby, or someone who sounds as though he could be Frisby, has been fixed with a passage to Buenos Aires, on a boat called the *Callida* which sails from Cardiff a week today."

"Where did they get this information?"

"A steward overheard a discussion between a woman and the second mate. Later he ran foul of the mate and got sacked, and decided he'd get his own back by squealing to the police about the deal."

"Has any action been taken yet?"

"No, Sir. The *Callida* is being kept under observation. Of course, but nothing more."

"What we need to do is to make sure that the expected passenger *is* Frisby. Did you manage to get a picture of his sister?"

"Yes, Sir. The Essex County Police found a photographer in Epping who took her picture a year ago for a passport."

Sergeant Southgate produced an envelope from his pocket with the air of a conjuror producing a rabbit out of a hat.

"There you are, Sir! One dozen copies, by express delivery this morning!"

"May we see, Uncle?" asked an eager Fluff.

Uncle Charles and the Sergeant grinned. "Nosey crew! Here, look at these!"

He put one of the newly arrived pictures on the table, and laid against it a photograph of Frisby. The family likeness was striking. Both had closely set eyes, long narrow noses, and hard mouths with thin lips.

"Gosh, Uncle!" exclaimed John. "They might be twins."

"Are they, sir?"

"No, Sergeant, she's probably a year or two older than her brother, but she could pass for him quite easily dressed in men's clothes."

Sergeant Southgate looked thoughtful for a moment, and then he grasped what his superior must have had in mind. "The Dublin business . . . ?"

"Yes, I think if we were to check her movements we might find they included a quick flight to Ireland and back. While she was there she could have changed into a man's suit and let herself be seen and reported upon. Then, before things got too hot, she would have changed back again and returned to Epping as herself."

"It looks, Sir, as though she may well be playing a very active part in the set-up."

"I would say it was highly likely. With this photo we

can soon find out if she was involved at Cardiff."

"By checking it with the steward?"

"Yes, Sergeant. We'll take a quick trip down to Cardiff today. If the steward is able to identify the woman from the picture, there's one very important thing we can then do . . ."

He paused, and Sergeant Southgate asked, "And that is?"

"Stop the fox's earth, Sergeant, stop the fox's earth! We can set a nice little trap for Frisby so that if he escapes us here, he will walk right into our net in Cardiff."

The next ten minutes were spent in making plans for the day. Uncle Charles and the Sergeant were to drive to Cardiff in Uncle Charles's car, dropping Fluff and John in Dolgelley to take the bus into Barmouth.

Fluff had protested, "But can't we come to Cardiff, too?"

Uncle Charles shook his head. "No. Quite definitely, no!"

He then pointed out that it was a long journey, and that Fluff and John couldn't very well be present when the steward was interviewed. "Why not enjoy yourselves in the sea? We'll pick you up at the Sergeant's hotel at about seven o'clock and have a quick meal, and then we'll see if Miss Bretherton is back."

Sergeant Southgate looked at his superior closely, and asked, "Do you think she will come back?"

"Yes, Sergeant, I do. And when we've talked to her, I've a hunch that several pieces of our jigsaw puzzle are going to drop very neatly into place."

Fluff and John had to be satisfied with that, but after

they had been dropped with their swimming gear in Dolgelley to wait for the Barmouth bus, they looked at each other glumly in depressed silence.

The only thing Fluff could find to say was, "It jolly well isn't fair. They're getting all the fun."

Little did they know, just then, that they were to find that it was much more exciting to chase a fox than to stop the fox's earth.

Chapter Eleven

At the Rainbow's End

The fox they found to chase turned out to be a vixen.

As they stepped off the bus in Barmouth, John grabbed Fluff's arm quite painfully. "Look!" he cried.

"Where?" queried the startled Fluff.

"Over there. Over the road! By the other bus stop . . . See?"

It was a busy street, crowded with gaily clad holiday-makers and noisy children. For a moment Fluff could not see what it was that was causing John's excitement.

Then her heart gave a sudden leap. "It's *her*, John. It's her! I'm positive!"

Buss Frisby's sister was far too busy with her own

thoughts to notice the sudden interest shown by the two youngsters who had just alighted from the bus on the other side of the street. Why, she wondered, had Evans telephoned her? He had sounded quite cheerful – unusual for him – and his cautiously worded message: *"The goods you ordered Madam, have been safely delivered as directed"*, clearly indicated that the visit to Buss had been troublefree. He had then suggested, *"If Madam could spare the time to meet me this morning, I could take her to inspect some curious and rather valuable pieces that she might like to add to her collection."*

The mystery was that the meeting place had been fixed, not at the shop, but at a tearoom in Llanelltyd on the Barmouth to Dolgelley road.

A bus drew up at her stop, and began to discharge its load of passengers.

"What are we going to do?" asked Fluff.

"Follow her," said John. "We'll stick like glue, and see where she leads us."

Several people had already joined the queue, and John and Fluff mingled with them, but, at John's suggestion, they got on the bus separately and sat apart. Miss Frisby took a front seat and started to read a newspaper.

The conductor came round to collect fares as the bus moved off, and Fluff wondered what she should do. In books, people who shadowed other people never seemed to be faced with this kind of problem. She was much too far back to hear what Miss Frisby had asked for, and for a moment, as the conductor reached her, she was panic-stricken.

"Where to, Miss?"

"Er, er . . . " she gulped, and then plunged, "Dolgelley please," and handed over a fifty pence piece.

Fortunately John heard her and asked for the same destination, but he began to worry what would happen if the bus went on beyond Dolgelley taking Miss Frisby with it.

It was a pleasant ride from Barmouth. The road ran along by the side of the Mawddach Estuary, and twisted and turned, weaving like a narrow ribbon along the steep hillside. On this particular morning the scenery was at its best. The brilliant sun, pouring down its warmth from a cloudless sky, made the blue waters sparkle and the yellow sands shimmer in a haze of heat. The distant mountains were clear and bright, and the massive Cader Idris lay outstretched like a basking giant.

"It must be wonderful to live here always. There couldn't be a nicer place," thought Fluff. But she found herself wondering what she wanted to do most – go detecting, go swimming or go for a walk with Willybach.

The thought of Willybach made her sad. Soon they would return to London, and then to school. Even if Uncle Charles and John could be persuaded to return to Wales next summer, that was a long, long time away, and Willybach would have forgotten her by then.

She began to think of persuading Uncle Charles to let her buy the dog. After all, Mr Jones did say he was hopeless as a sheepdog and couldn't earn his keep on the farm. She had got about four pounds in the Post Office. John owed her ninety pence, and she was pretty certain there was at least another ninety pence in the piggy bank on her dressing table in the Kensington flat. She opened her purse. There were three ten pence pieces, two five pence pieces, several pennies and a rather sticky, fluff-covered toffee. She defluffed the toffee and popped it into her mouth, and while chewing, calculated her wealth. It came to over six pounds. Surely that was enough to buy Willybach.

She was roused from her day-dream by the slowing down of the bus, and she saw Miss Frisby get to her feet. A sign by the roadside said that the cluster of houses they were approaching was Llanelltyd.

John, alert as always, had already spotted the woman's intention of leaving the bus. He made a point of being in front of her at the door as the vehicle stopped. A moment later, and without so much as a backward glance, he was down the steps and striding towards the little Post Office, just as though he had business there.

Miss Frisby hesitated for a moment on the pavement, and an agitated Fluff bumped into her from behind. "Sorry," she muttered, and then to cover her confusion, bent down pretending to adjust her sandal strap.

When Fluff looked up again, Miss Frisby had walked away towards a teashop where a signboard announced, *MORNING COFFEE NOW BEING SERVED.*

The bus, with its somewhat puzzled conductor, was already rolling away on noisy gears towards Dolgelley. As it drew out into the middle of the road to pass a parked van, Fluff gasped. There was something very familiar about that van. It was old and a very rusty green! She quickly ran to join John, who had moved out of sight round the corner of the Post Office.

In the café Evans greeted Miss Frisby pleasantly enough, but immediately the solitary waitress had disappeared to fetch two coffees he asked, "You're sure you've not been followed?"

Miss Frisby shook her head. "No, there wasn't a sign of anyone. A couple of kids got off the bus, that was all."

Evans moved quickly to the door and looked out ino the street. It was deserted. He resumed his seat and queried, "Two kids?"

"Yes, two kids; a boy and a clumsy idiot of a girl." Miss Frisby was puzzled. "What's got into you?"

Evans persisted with his questioning: "Were they together?"

"No, not as far as I could see. But why worry about a couple of kids?"

"You gave me a bit of a fright. I thought for a moment they might be Frost's brats."

Miss Frisby leant over the table and took a cigarette from the packet by Evans's plate. As she tapped it on the table, she said, "You've got Frost on the brain. You don't need to worry about him. He got kicked out of the Force ages ago."

Coffee was brought in, and both were silent for a while. Then Miss Frisby asked, "What about you? Are you certain you weren't tailed?"

"I haven't seen anybody, and I've kept my eyes skinned, so I reckon we're safe enough for a while, providing we're careful."

He waited for his companion to finish her coffee and then rang the bell for the waitress, in order to pay the bill.

When they got to the van and were seated, Miss Frisby asked, "Well, what do you want me for? Got the money sooner than you thought?"

Evans pressed the starter button and the engine spluttered into life. "No," he answered, "I haven't. That won't be here until tomorrow, and I'll give it to you as arranged. It's not about that. I wanted to talk to you because I did a lot of thinking last night."

The van jerked slowly away and, to the woman's surprise, and the surprise and consternation of the two observers, almost immediately turned into a side road. This led away from the village and wound steeply up the wooded hillside.

"What were you thinking about?"

Evans changed to his lowest gear, and the engine noise made it difficult for her to hear his reply. "About you and Buss. I reckon neither of you will let me alone until you get what you're after. Well you're going to get it!"

The road was clear of the trees now, and on the right was a bare rocky slope, with a few sheep grazing here and there.

"We get out here!" announced Evans, as he pulled up by a narrow bridge. "And walk!"

Miss Frisby retorted, "I'm not walking anywhere until you tell me what this is all about."

"Well," said Evans, "I've had enough. Look what's happened so far. There we were, sitting pretty on a fortune, when that fool brother of yours shoots off his mouth and Frost picks us up. We might easily have got 'life' over that. That was half the gold gone, and the other half, my share, could have gone the same way too."

The woman interrupted him. "But it didn't. Buss kept quiet, and I kept quiet. Anyway, I could easily have stepped in and moved it while you were both in clink. Buss let on to me that you'd got the stuff buried in the floor of a hut on your uncle's farm."

"You might have found it, and you might not. Buss couldn't have seen much that night. It was as black as pitch. Anyway, you didn't move it; I did. And I put it where no one could find it. But that's finished with. I've taken out all I want, about another twenty thousand poundsworth, and the rest is yours."

The woman regarded him suspiciously. "Why? What's the catch?"

"I told you. I've had enough of you and Buss. If you'd left it to me, I'd have seen you were both all right."

Evans looked at her fiercely, and continued, "Haven't I kept you going with money since I got out?"

"Yes – chickenfeed," she sneered. "It helped Buss get away, and now he's free we can both twist your arm."

Evans lit a cigarette with shaking fingers. "All right, you've twisted my arm and I've had enough. You can do what you like with the rest, only leave me in peace."

He pointed to the hill. "It's up there!"

She looked at him in astonishment. "Up where?"

"Up there!" He pointed at a group of rocks about fifty yards away. "That's the entrance to an old gold mine." He gave a rueful chuckle, and added, "I put more gold in there, I reckon, than was ever brought out of it!"

Evans got out of the van. "Do you want to see where I put it?"

Miss Frisby's eyes glittered, bright with greed. "Yes, show me."

She followed him eagerly up the hill.

John and Fluff stared in astonishment as the van left the main road of Llanelltyd, and turned right on to the narrow winding hill road.

"What does your map show?" asked Fluff. "Where does that road go to?"

"Nowhere in particular," announced John. And with his finger he traced the slim yellow line through a green wooded patch to where it came to an abrupt halt in a maze of red contour lines. An unfenced track led from there to a lonely farm, and just before the road ended, it showed a bridge over a small stream.

"Let's follow," said John. "It's only about a mile to the end of the road proper, and the farm track is about another mile long at the most."

They started off by running a few yards and walking a

few yards, but the steep hill soon slowed them down.

"I can't keep up!" gasped Fluff. "I just can't."

"It's not much further," said John, reassuringly. "In a moment we'll be out of the trees."

At the edge of the wood he stopped and crouched down by the roadside.

Thankfully Fluff slumped down beside him. "I'm beat!"

"Look!" John parted the bracken for her. "Up the road!"

The deserted van stood just off the road by the bridge. "That's the bridge Miss Bretherton painted!" exclaimed Fluff. "It's like the picture Uncle bought from her. There's the dead twisted tree, too."

"Didn't you tell me that Mr Jones mentioned something about an old gold mine when he was looking at the painting?"

"Yes, he did," said Fluff. "I'm sure he did."

"Then," reasoned John, "I wouldn't mind betting that the opening to it is among those rocks over there. Anyway it should be, according to the map. See, it's marked *Disused Mine.*"

"I wonder where they've got to?" Fluff cupped her ear in her hand. "Can you hear anything?"

They both listened intently for a few moments. But beyond the murmuring and splashing of the stream over its stony bed, and the occasional call of a sheep, there was nothing.

"My guess is that they've both gone down the mine," said John. "I vote we hide under the bridge so that we are really close to them when they come back to the van."

They made a quick dash for the bridge and scrambled down the bank and out of sight.

It was only now, as they waited in silence, that they realised the weather was changing rapidly. A sudden cold, gusty wind was filling the summer sky with sullen clouds. From the far distance came the first growling rumbles of thunder.

The further they proceeded down the steeply sloping mineshaft, the more suspicious and dubious Miss Frisby became.

Evans had produced a torch, and its flickering light gleamed on the damp walls and occasionally lit up the massive beams of rotting timber which supported the roof.

It was cold, too, and the woman shivered in her thin summer dress. "How much further?" she called. Her voice echoed and re-echoed eerily.

"Not very far," replied Evans. "We have to take a shaft to the right here. See this mark on the corner?"

He held the torch so that she could see a crude *E* chalked on the flat rock surface.

The side-shaft opened up into a small rock chamber. "Now you hold the torch," commanded Evans. "Point it this way."

He began to move loose stones from a pile in the corner. Buried underneath were some small wooden boxes. When one had been fully uncovered, he lifted it out to the centre of the floor. It was very heavy for its size.

"Now I'll show you what's inside." Evans had come prepared with a sturdy screwdriver and with it he broke the sealed wire band securing the lid. Inside the box were two ingots which glistened almost evilly in the torchlight.

Miss Frisby's hands were shaking as she reached down to touch the metal.

"Well," said Evans, "there it is, and a lot of good may it do you."

She gave a harsh, low chuckle. "I'll be the best judge of that!" she declared. Then, playing the torch over the remainder of the partly exposed heap, she asked, "How many boxes?"

"Fourteen," answered Evans. "And, at current market prices, they're worth in all nearly a quarter of a million quid. If you unload it steadily – but I don't suppose either of you will have sense enough to do that – you ought to get about half that figure."

Miss Frisby laughed again. "That'll do for me," she said. "That's more than a hundred thousand smackers."

She kicked the lid back into place with her foot. "Aren't you going to put it back for me?"

Evans replaced the box with unusual care, reaching down behind another box to adjust a small switch. He used similar caution in putting back the covering of rocks, but the woman was too obsessed with her own thoughts to notice his slow and deliberate actions.

"Will that do for you?" he asked as he straightened his back.

"That'll do," she said. "They won't be there long. Buss will soon help me move 'em, and I think we'll be cancelling that little trip over the water."

"I think you will too," muttered Evans as he led the way out of the chamber into the main shaft.

The sudden summer storm brought with it a cloud-burst, and the water in the stream rose rapidly and angrily as every rill on the hillside fed rainwater into it.

"I hope they won't be much longer," said John, "otherwise we're going to be washed away!"

Fluff, crouching well up the bank, was too wet, cold and miserable to make a reply. Although she hated to admit it, even to herself, the thunder had been quite frightening as it rolled and echoed among the hills.

Quite suddenly they heard footsteps stumbling among the rocks nearby. The woman was cursing profusely as the van door was hurriedly opened and slammed shut again. In the same moment the engine started and the vehicle lurched away.

Long before John had scrambled to the top of the bank the road was empty. Fluff joined him, feeling glad that she could stretch her cramped legs again.

"All that wet wait for nothing!" exclaimed John, in disgust.

A few moments later the rain began to ease off, and the sun broke through the clouds. With the sun the great arch of a brilliant rainbow spread across the hill-side. It seemed very close, and one end wrapped the cluster of rocks at the mine entrance in transparent glory.

Fluff forgot her misery and clapped her hands with excitement. "John! John!" she shouted, "The crock of gold! The crock of gold! We've found the gold!"

Chapter Twelve

Down the Mine

In her excitement, Fluff insisted that they ought to go down the mine.

John said, "No," but not as firmly as he should have. It would be fun to find the gold and take a bar back to Uncle Charles to prove they had found it. Fluff argued. "We must, John, we must!"

John made another feeble protest. "We haven't got a torch."

Fluff's face fell. She looked most woebegone.

"I've got a box of matches," said John, relenting. He produced a rather battered, and only partly full box from the hip pocket of his shorts. "Promise you'll come back quickly if we start running out of matches. It could be awfully dangerous down there without a light."

Fluff promised readily enough. This was a real adventure. It was almost as good as *Treasure Island*.

"Come on then, and don't squeal if you get mixed up with bats or rats or spiders."

"Of course I won't squeal. You know I won't!"

They had gone only a few yards down the shaft, when a sharp turn to the right meant they were shut off from the daylight.

The first match was struck, but it went out almost at once. "These matches are damp," complained John, "and so is the box. It's a job to strike them."

He tried again, this time with more success, and they got several yards further without difficulty.

Now it was Fluff who was getting worried. It was all right being brave outside, but down here, where it was so black and damp and cold, she didn't feel quite the same. The drip, drip, drip from the roof held a menacing sound, and the glimpse she had caught of the rotted and twisted roof timbers had been rather frightening.

John struck another match. It showed that the shaft was descending rapidly, and that there were lots of loose stones which they could easily fall over without a proper light. But John did not hesitate, and while the match lasted, he led the way forward and downward.

Fluff's courage was giving out rapidly. "I don't like it, John," she said in a shivery voice, as they stood together in the darkness between matches. He fumbled for another match as she continued, "Don't you think we had better go back?"

"Not yet, Fluff. I've still got plenty of matches left."

Another match flared into light, and Fluff could see her brother peering forward into the gloom. "Come on! It looks as though there's a side shaft along here. I bet that's where old Evans has hidden the gold."

Once more they moved forward, and they reached the side shaft just as the match burnt down to John's fingers. He dropped it hurriedly. "Ouch! That hurt!"

Fluff heard him sucking at the burns. "Hurry up, John. Let's have a quick look and get out of here. It's spooky!"

"You promised not to squeal – remember?"

"I *haven't* squealed, but I don't promise I won't unless we get out quickly."

"Girls!" said John in disgust, and began to feel in his box for another match.

There was an ominous 'plop' as he dropped the box and it fell into a pool of water.

"Suffering Moses!" he exclaimed. "That's torn it. I've dropped the matches!"

Fluff was already groping for them. "They're in the water," she wailed. "Now what do we do?"

"We go back," said John. "Just as you wanted. But it's a pity . . . I bet we can almost put our hands on the gold where we are right now."

"I don't care about the gold," stated Fluff firmly. "I just want to see the daylight again."

She turned to lead the way back. John hesitated for a moment and then followed her. It wasn't until much later that John and Fluff were to learn how the mishap with the dropped matches had saved their lives.

Still clutching the useless wet box, John took the lead in the slow, painful return to the surface. It seemed to

be an endless climb, stumbling over loose stones and bumping into rough walls, before they turned the last corner but one and saw a faint glimmer of reflected daylight.

"Hooray!" shouted John. "We've made it!"

Fluff gave a huge sigh of relief. "Gosh!" she said with feeling. "I wouldn't want to go through that again. Fancy dropping the matches, just when we wanted them most!"

This brought only a snort from John, as he quickened the pace upward.

The full light of day was almost too painful to bear, and for a little while they stood together at the entrance to the mine blinking their eyes.

"I reckon we ought to get back to Dolgelley," said John. "But we must get ourselves cleaned up a bit first. You should see yourself!"

"What about you?" retorted Fluff, pushing her bedraggled hair out of her face with a muddy hand. "You're just as mucky as I am – worse probably."

"We can wash in the stream," suggested John. "We've got all our bathing towels and things in your bucket bag under the bridge."

"And there are some biscuits, and cheese rolls in the bag too," announced Fluff, "and two apples. I pushed them in before we left in case we got hungry on the beach."

"I'm hungry now," said John. "Lead me to them!"

Later, after they had cleaned themselves up and combed their hair, they sat down on the parapet of the bridge and thankfully tucked into the food Fluff had provided.

Pointing up at the mine entrance with his half eaten apple John declared with feeling, "I wouldn't go down that shaft again without proper lights, and a spare torch as well, for all the tea in China."

"Nor would I," agreed Fluff, "for all the gold in the Bank of England!"

Chapter Thirteen

Leonie Returns and Fluff Disappears

It was Sergeant Southgate who first spotted the two figures trudging wearily over the bridge into Dolgelley through the gently falling rain.

"Isn't that Fiona and John?" he asked.

His superior took a quick look, and, having glanced in his mirror to see that no other car was close behind, he drew up to the pavement beside the weary pair. "Get in you two. You look like a couple of half drowned ducks!"

Fluff sank exhausted into the back seat and John flung himself in beside her. "That's a bit of luck," he said. "I thought I'd end up by carrying her. We missed the blessed bus!"

"But what a day!" cried Fluff in ecstasy. "What a fabulous, fabulous day! We've found the gold, Uncle. We've really found the gold. I'm sure we know where it's hidden!"

Long-suffering Uncle Charles and the disbelieving Sergeant Southgate gave vent to a long mock groan in chorus. "Oh no! Not again!"

Both were smiling. But their smiles ceased when John, frequently interrupted by the irrepressible Fluff, told the story of their day's adventures.

"You should have had more sense, John," said Uncle Charles sharply, "than to take Fluff down that mine-shaft. These old mines are terribly dangerous and for all you knew, Evans and the Frisby woman might have come back."

Fluff wasn't going to let John take all the blame. "I made him do it, Uncle," she admitted. "But I soon wished I hadn't."

"Oughtn't I to go straight back and get a guard put on the mine entrance?" asked the Sergeant as the car came to a halt alongside the caravan. "There's obviously something odd about the place and, rainbow or no rainbow, it is possible the gold may be hidden in it."

"Inside you two, and get yourselves dry," Uncle Charles commanded the youngsters. "We'll talk here in the car while you are changing and then we'll have a hot cup of tea."

He then turned to deal with the Sergeant's suggestion. "Yes, Sergeant, I think we should get a couple of men up there as quickly as possible, and also make arrangements for a thorough search. That may take time. Some of those old mines have got all kinds of side shafts, and it could be days before we find anything. But there's one thing we must certainly do right away, and that is tighten our grip on Evans. We'll also spread the net for Frisby and his sister."

"You don't want to pull them in now, Sir?"

"No, not yet. Let's make sure we're on to the gold first. It certainly looks as though we may be this time, but I still have a hunch that Evans has got something up his sleeve." He went on, "I'm really grateful to those two nosey parkers of mine. They did a good job, but I dread to think of the consequences if they had fallen foul of Evans and his pal."

By this time John and Fluff had changed, and Fluff came out with a bundle of wet clothing to hang on the line strung at the back of the caravan. "John's putting the kettle on, Uncle," she announced.

"You'd better have a cup of tea, Sergeant, before you go," invited Uncle Charles, leading the way into the caravan. "And we'll go over the next moves again just to make sure that there is no possibility of a slip up."

But before they could settle down to their tea, a car was heard approaching by the farm track. It was Miss Bretherton's mini.

Fluff opened the door to her, and Leonie stepped inside. "Hello," she said cheerily. "Mr Jones tells me I'm on your wanted list, Inspector!"

Uncle Charles said gruffly and officially, "I think you owe us an explanation young woman, and the sooner you make it the better for all of us."

Leonie was smiling, and Fluff decided that she was very pretty. Sergeant Southgate thought the same and after the introductions were made he offered her his seat.

"I certainly owe you an apology," she replied. "You see, for a short time, Inspector Frost, I was almost convinced you were in league with Evans and Frisby, and that this holiday was just a blind. It seemed a good cover for a meeting in which the three of you could get together and split what was left of the E.&A. gold shipment."

The look of indignation on Uncle Charles's face was almost comic, and Fluff was sure he was about to explode.

Leonie, however, carried on with a most disarming

smile. "After all, and you've just got to admit it, there have been crooked policemen before now, and it was hard to believe that your being here was only a coincidence."

Once again Uncle Charles threatened to erupt, but Leonie added hurriedly, "This, I think, will help with the explanation!"

She produced from her handbag a cellophane-protected card. On one side it carried a photograph which was far from flattering. On the other side was an authority and a description of herself. She placed the card on the table. The authority read – and Fluff was well forward for a quick look at it:

Miss Leonie Bretherton,
Claims Investigation Department,
International Bullion Insurance Ltd,
Cornhill, London, E.C.1.

Then followed particulars of height, weight, colour of eyes and date of birth. The latter set Fluff and the lanky Sergeant Southgate doing some quick mental arithmetic.

Uncle Charles's wrath subsided with the production of this card, and he listened intently as Leonie completed her story.

Apparently her insurance company had been stirred into opening another series of investigations when it was reported that Frisby had escaped from Dartmoor. The loss of the quarter of a million pounds paid out in this case still rankled, and it was not going to be written off in a hurry. Leonie had been assigned to the job.

She said, "I was certain that Frisby would try to contact Evans if the gold was still around, and the old papers gave me a lead to Evans's possible whereabouts. They mentioned his only known relative, an old boy who owned Caffryn-Mawr. It was a lucky break for me. Within two days I'd got on the trail of Evans through Mr Jones, and settled down to watch him at his shop." She paused to accept a cup of tea from John.

"That was easy for me of course. Painting is a useful hobby, and a wonderful cover if you want to spend a long time watching anything or anyone. You can do it so obviously."

Uncle Charles nodded agreement, and Leonie continued, "I found a corner by the supermarket from which I could get a good view of the shop, and settled down to work on the painting you saw up at the farm. Although I was pestered frequently by visitors, all trying to see what I had on my canvas, the watching was well worth it – or, at least I thought so." She paused to sip her tea.

"Frisby's sister appeared on several occasions and behaved in a most peculiar manner. It looked to me as though she was either watching the shop too, or keeping guard. I wondered for a time if Frisby was hidden up there. Later I decided that Evans wouldn't have been fool enough to take a chance like that. Anyway, if she was watching Evans she missed the vital move. Late one afternoon, just about closing time, he loaded a number of boxes into his van. As soon as I saw what he was up to, I packed my painting gear and stationed the mini where I could start tailing the van whenever it moved off."

Again she paused. Fluff was bursting with impatience.

"I was absolutely determined to see what was in

those boxes. They looked exactly like the E.&A. bullion cases at a distance. So I followed him – out of the town and then along the Barmouth road as far as Llanelltyd."

Only a severe, warning look and Uncle Charles's raised finger stopped Fluff from interrupting.

"At Llanelltyd, the van turned up a side road. This made things tricky, and I had to move with considerable care after this. Fortunately, I spotted the van pulled up by the roadside before I broke out from the tree-covered part of the road. I left the car there and then went forward in the shadows to see what he was up to."

"And there he was," said Uncle Charles, "taking the boxes into an old mineshaft."

It was Leonie's turn to look astonished. "How did you know about the mineshaft?" she asked.

"Carry on, Miss Bretherton. It was very wrong of me to break in. I'll tell you our side of the story in a moment."

"Well really, Inspector! But I'll carry on with the report to its rather sad ending." She sipped her tea again.

"I reckoned, then, that the best thing for me to do was to get out of the way whilst he finished the job, and to go back later when the coast was clear to have a look at the boxes in the shaft."

"Did you?"

"Yes, I did. I went into the village and bought two torches . . . " Here Uncle Charles gave an approving nod at her forethought. "And after I'd seen Evans's van return to Dolgelley, I went back to the mine."

"Did you find the boxes?"

"Yes, quite easily. They are, or were, packed away

under some loose stones in a chamber away from the main shaft."

Fluff's wild surge of enthusiasm and excitement was rapidly draining away. "No gold?" she asked sadly.

"No gold," confirmed Miss Bretherton. "Two of the top boxes contained brass ingots; the others were empty. I checked all of them. Some were sealed rather like the E.&A. boxes, but there was no gold. I replaced everything as I had found it and went back to my car to think."

"And where did that lead you?" asked Sergeant Southgate.

"Precisely nowhere. I decided to keep a watch on the place for a day or two, but out of sight this time."

"Was that when you did my painting?" asked Uncle Charles.

"Yes. That was painted from a spot tucked nicely away in the trees and fifty yards from the road. When Evans returned two days later he didn't spot me although he looked round pretty carefully. This time he only took one box down the shaft."

"And what did that contain?"

"I didn't need to go down the mine to find that out. I could read through my field glasses what was stencilled on the side of the box. There were two words: GELIGNITE and DANGEROUS."

"Gosh!" exclaimed Fluff and John.

"So that's where the quarry explosives went!" concluded Sergeant Southgate.

Uncle Charles addressed John and Fluff. "You are a lucky pair of young idiots! If you hadn't dropped that box of matches you might both be dead and buried by now. If you'd touched those boxes, my guess is you'd have been blown to smithereens."

Fluff shivered. This revelation had left her, for once, speechless. It was Uncle Charles who had to explain to Leonie about the day's adventures.

Leonie shook her head gravely. "I wish now I had reported this mine business to someone earlier. I didn't think for a moment that anyone except Evans and Frisby would be likely to use that shaft."

"If either of those two got blown up, it wouldn't jolly well matter," John said with feeling.

Leonie went on with the account of her activities.

Feeling that little more could come from watching the mineshaft, she had turned her attention to Caffryn-Mawr. There, after a search, she had found the first of the lead seals and knew she had one tangible clue, at least, to the whereabouts of the missing gold. The arrival of Uncle Charles with John and Fluff had complicated matters considerably. The bearded man who had also appeared could, she thought, be none other than Frisby, and the idea of a conspiracy began to enter her mind.

"When I was introduced to you on the morning Fluff fell into the sheep-dip tank, the name Frost vaguely meant something to me. I made an excuse about going off for paint, and checked up with my head office. What they told me set me thinking furiously. The man in charge of the original investigations had been a certain Chief Inspector Frost – a man who had since left the police service and had a noticeable limp!"

"And so you had the audacity to link me with Frisby and Evans in a share-out of the loot I'd supposedly failed to recover?"

Leonie smiled very sweetly and said meekly, "Yes, Inspector. But I do hope I'm forgiven now. And I suppose I owe you an apology for going through your things in the caravan."

"You most certainly do!"

"It was then that I found a note which cleared you completely. In it you referred to the sending of the horse brass to Scotland Yard for a fingerprint test. I did try to make amends before I went to London, yesterday, to make my report and get instructions about co-operating with you and the police."

"By leaving me the two seals?"

"Yes. I think they do give us a definite lead, and prove almost conclusively that the gold was brought to this farm."

"It certainly does look like it. But there's still one other thing which needs clearing up."

"And what is that, Inspector?"

"What were you doing prowling about here on Monday night?"

Leonie shook her head. "That wasn't me; I can assure you of that. There had been a woman about that evening, or during the night, because I found some cigarette ends in the hut on the hill when I returned on the Tuesday morning. One of the ends was stained with lipstick in a shade quite different from mine. It was an orange tinge that I'd hate to use."

"Miss Frisby!" declared Fluff. "She was wearing that kind of lipstick when we saw her today!" She appealed to John for confirmation. "Wasn't she?"

John agreed, but a little uncertainly. "I think so. But I didn't notice all that particularly."

With the explanations completed, and aware now of the extent of Leonie's investigations to date, Uncle Charles and Sergeant Southgate began to discuss plans for pulling in Evans and the Frisby pair. They at once came into conflict with Leonie.

"My interests and yours aren't quite the same," she pointed out. "My main concern is the recovery of the gold. Can't we give Evans a day or two more in which to make a move?"

The argument that followed was too technical to be of interest to John and Fluff, so they went off to wash up the teacups, until a decision was reached.

"Get some water, please, Fluff," said John. "We're right out."

Fluff opened the door and looked out on to a wet and dreary scene of sodden grass, dripping trees and grey, writhing mist creeping down the hillside. She felt a strong urge to argue the matter, and appeal to John's better nature. It was, anyhow, his turn to go for water. Then she decided it would lead to a waste of time if they had a battle and, reluctantly, she pulled on her wellingtons and grabbed a raincoat.

Five minutes later she had still not returned and an impatient John went to look for her. All he found at the water point was a blue plastic bucket rolling among the small rocks in the turbulent stream.

Three times he called her name. There was no reply; only the noise of the tumbling water and the dripping of the rain from the trees.

Uncle Charles was on his feet as soon as he saw the boy's haggard white face at the door.

"Fluff's disappeared!" cried John, "I can't find her anywhere!"

Chapter Fourteen

Kidnapped!

Fluff looked at the swollen stream with distaste and hoped it hadn't risen so much that it would overtop her wellingtons. "John's mean, jolly mean," she said to herself indignantly, as she stepped carefully from the bank and held her bucket under the waterfall. It really was his turn to fetch the water, and she intended to have it out with him the first time they were on their own. Much of her annoyance came from the fact that she might be missing something back at the caravan, while John was there in the thick of the excitement. "Brothers!" she snorted in disgust.

The bucket filled rapidly and she straightened up to lift it to the bank.

A sudden sound behind her caught her completely off guard, and a moment later, a large hand was clamped over her mouth while an arm pinioned her arms and waist. "One squeak out of you, and I'll knock your head in!"

Fluff dropped the bucket as she was swung violently up the bank and carried into the trees. They were some distance from the caravan before she was put on her feet. Before her mouth was uncovered, the same gruff voice repeated the threat: "I'm telling you – one squeak and I'll bash your head in."

It was the bearded man. "Buss Frisby!" ejaculated Fluff.

"You know that, do you, little nosey?" Frisby grabbed her by her arm and forced her, half running half walking, up the hillside beside him. "We'll soon find out what else you know."

Long before John had raised the alarm, Frisby and his captive were well out of sight over the shoulder of the hill, and making for the lower slopes of the mountain.

Fluff will never forget that awful journey, stumbling and falling over the rocks. Once Frisby lost the way and they nearly staggered over the edge of an old quarry. The only time Frisby spoke was to curse the swirling mists, or to threaten her if she slackened her pace. Never once did he lose his hold on her arm.

At last they arrived at a shepherd's shelter which, Fluff guessed, must be Frisby's hideout. He pushed her inside and flung her on to a heap of blankets in the corner. After making the door secure and blocking the solitary window, Frisby lit a small paraffin lamp.

Fluff, who felt a bit sick, had a quick look round while her gaoler lit a cigarette. The shelter was tiny, no more than six feet square at the most. Half the floor was covered with rough boards to make a sleeping place, and the rest was earth and rock. It was damp and cold and smelled fusty.

On the ledge half way up the wall, originally intended to hold bottles of sheep medicines and ointments, Frisby had arranged, in surprisingly neat order, some tins of soup and meat, biscuits, milk and cheese. A packet of sugar had been partly torn open and was spilling over. One niche in the thick wall held a primus stove, another, a small transistor radio.

Secure in the hut, and with a cigarette between his lips, Frisby became less aggressive. Even so, as he towered high above her, Fluff could feel the black menace of his ill-concealed ferocity.

"Answer my questions and I won't hurt you. Lie to me and you'll regret it. Now sit up so I can see your face."

Fluff sat up reluctantly, and Frisby held the lamp so that the light was bright in her eyes.

"Are you Frost's kid?"

"Mr Frost is my uncle."

"What's he doing here?"

"We're on holiday."

Frisby raised his hand to strike her. "You know what I said? No lies now!"

"It's true! We came down here on holiday!"

A heavy blow caught the side of Fluff's face and knocked her sideways into the blankets. Rough hands pulled her back into a sitting position, dazed and a little tearful. She was, however, more angry than frightened, and lashed out at the man's shins with her foot. Her wellingtons spoilt the effect of the blow.

Oddly enough, Frisby laughed and let go of her. "You've got a bit of spirit, kid, haven't you?"

"I wasn't telling lies!" declared Fluff. "We did come here on holiday. We didn't know about you, or Evans, or anybody, and I wish we had never come now!"

Frisby sat down heavily beside her. "O.K., so you did come here for a holiday." He then shot out, "Why?"

"We were just looking for a caravan site and we found this. Mr Jones said we could stay and we paid him a pound."

"Who is this Mr Jones? The farmer who comes up to the yard sometimes?"

"Yes."

Frisby swore unpleasantly. "How much does your Uncle Frost know now? And don't lie to me! I know he's been in Evans's shop."

This was difficult for Fluff to answer, and she hesitated.

Frisby warned her again, "No lies now!" Then he made the answers more easy to find by continuing with direct questions.

"Does he know I've been living at the farm?"

"Yes."

"How?"

"We saw you the day we arrived."

"How did you know it was me?"

"We found your fingerprint on a piece of horse brass in Mr Evans's shop. Uncle Charles had it checked by Scotland Yard, and he put two and two together and decided it was you we'd seen up at the farm."

It had occurred to Fluff that there was no point in telling Frisby that it was she who had identified him from his picture. He seemed satisfied with the explanation, although he had sworn again when she mentioned the fingerprint on the brass.

"Is the farm being watched? No lies or you'll get another clout!"

"I don't think so. I do know the roads and the stations are being patrolled."

Frisby cursed again. "What about that painting woman? Who is she?"

"She paints pictures. Her name's Leonie Bretherton."

This time Fluff was purposely stupid, and Frisby looked at her suspiciously. "She's not connected with the cops?"

"No, she's just a painter. Uncle bought one of her pictures."

After that Frisby was silent for quite a long time. Once he got up to look outside, and some of the grey mist seemed to creep through the open door. It was also getting dark. He muttered something under his breath which sounded to Fluff like, "No good, I'll have to wait for the morning."

Before he sat down he opened a tin of tomato soup and put this in a saucepan to heat. Fluff watched with interest as he pumped and lit the stove. "Here kid, you can stir it," he said, and gave her a spoon.

Fluff was only too glad to be allowed to move and to have something to do.

"No tricks, mind!" Frisby watched her warily, and when the soup was hot enough he poured half of it into a mug and patted the blanket beside him. "Get the biscuits and sit down."

It was the strangest meal Fluff had ever eaten. She was given the mug, while Frisby supped his soup from the saucepan with the spoon. He shared out the biscuits, a few rather soft cream crackers, with scrupulous fairness. "I 'spect you're hungry."

Fluff said she was, and she felt even more hungry when she remembered she'd only had a snack during the day, and realised there wasn't much chance of getting a proper evening meal. But the soup was good and warm, and the biscuits helped to fill the hole where the inner Fluff should have been.

"Like some music?" asked her odd companion. He reached up for the little radio and turned the tuning dial. Eventually the haunting strains of *Stranger on the Shore* filled the hut.

"I like that," declared Frisby. "That's good music, that is."

"This is crazy," thought Fluff. "Here am I, sitting on a mountain side with an escaped convict who has kidnapped me, knocked me about, and now he wants to talk politely about music."

"I like it too," she replied. "I like Cliff Richard as well. Do you like him, Mr Frisby?"

It seemed that he did, and then he spoke of playing the saxophone. "I wish I'd kept it up," he said regretfully. "I reckon I could have been good at it by now."

At ten o'clock he turned to the news bulletin. Although Fluff's eyes were heavy with sleep and sore with the cigarette smoke in the small room, she listened intently, in case there was any mention of what the newspapers referred to as 'The Frisby Hunt'. There was. The announcer read:

> "The search for Frisby, the escaped Dartmoor prisoner, has been switched from Dublin to an area in North Wales. Police have been hampered tonight by heavy mists, but developments are expected tomorrow when troops from Territorial Army units in camps nearby will be used to assist in the search. An eleven year old girl, Fiona Carr, niece of Chief Inspector Frost, who is in charge of the Frisby Hunt, has been reported missing and it is feared that Frisby may be holding the child as a hostage."

Frisby looked at Fluff thoughtfully. "I hadn't calculated on that," he said. "You could be useful."

"You mean as a hostage, Mr Frisby?"

"Yep – I might be able to do a bit of bargaining with you."

Curiously enough, Fluff was no longer frightened of him. She felt, if anything, sorry for him in the same kind of way she might have felt sorry for a trapped animal, even if the animal was wild and vicious. Frisby, not knowing why he was doing it, was responding in the way in which animals were always going to respond to Fluff. Despite his threats, she knew he could never hurt her again.

"No!" he went on. "I don't think I will. I'll get away better on my own."

Still talking aloud to himself, he added, "I'd better get rid of this beard though. They'll be looking for a man with a beard."

He heated up a small quantity of water in the saucepan and then busied himself with scissors, soap and razor. The result seemed to please him and he rubbed his smooth chin with satisfaction.

The sleepy Fluff nodded agreement when he asked her approval.

"That's better isn't it?"

"Yes, Mr Frisby, much better."

"Right then, let's have some kip – " He paused. "I'm going outside for a minute, but if you want to, you can go first. Mind, don't go far away, it's dangerous."

Fluff was not embarrassed. She knew exactly what he meant and slipped quickly outside. It was pitch black and very cold. The crack of light from the partly closed door showed through the mist for only a few feet. It would have been madness to try to get away. Fluff reckoned that Frisby was just as much a prisoner as she was.

He smiled at her on her return. "O.K?"

"Yes, Mr Frisby, thank you."

This is crazy, thought Fluff, for a second time, completely crazy. This isn't a bit like it ought to be, or at least as the books say it is. But then nobody seems to think of that sort of thing in books.

There were four blankets in the hut, and Frisby gave two to Fluff and kept two for himself.

"It gets cold up here at night," he explained. "Keep your mac on and wrap yourself up in those. You can doss down in that corner. I'll keep the lamp going; it'll help a bit."

He stretched out partly across the door and partly across the boards. "Goodnight," he murmured, "I'm sorry I clouted you, kid, but I had to know."

"It's all right, Mr Frisby, goodnight."

Fluff went to sleep almost immediately, and Frisby, having made his plans for the morning, slept also.

When Fluff awoke, Frisby had gone. He had taken his leave quite silently and without disturbing her, even though he had dropped his two blankets over her and partly tucked them in. On a scrap of dirty paper, propped against the lamp, was a short message: DON'T MOVE TILL MIST GONE. KEEP THE TRANNY.

Fluff got up and looked outside. The grey light of morning was filtering through the woolly wet mist, but she couldn't see enough to find a path which would lead to safety.

Rummaging around among the tins on the ledge, she found three more limp biscuits and a small block of fruit and nut chocolate. Then she switched on the radio and went back to bed to enjoy her breakfast and morning music.

"The time," said the announcer, "is now six forty one."

Chapter Fifteen

Willybach to the Rescue

Two large, stolid policemen kept watch at the caravan that night. After the first fruitless search for Fluff, Uncle Charles insisted that Leonie take John to the Jones's farm to sleep, whilst he and Sergeant Southgate spent the night organising the big search which was to start at dawn.

Neither Leonie nor John slept well. At about four o'clock in the morning John tapped on Leonie's door, and found her wide awake and sitting up in bed.

"I've got an idea, Miss Bretherton."

"What, John?"

"Perhaps Willybach could find her?"

"I don't think so, John. He isn't the right kind of dog for that."

"But Willybach's fond of Fluff. Really fond of her. You know how she is with dogs!"

Leonie considered the matter for a moment, wishing all the time that she didn't have to cast a damper on the boy's hopes.

Disturbed by the sound of their voices, Mr and Mrs Jones appeared at the bedroom door wondering what was happening.

Leonie put John's suggestion to Mr Jones. "What do you think?"

Mr Jones shook his head, but Mrs Jones said, "Don't say no like that Gwylym, it might be worth trying."

Leonie turned to John. "We must take something of Fluff's from the caravan so that he can get a scent."

"Right, I'll get something."

"Well then," put in Mr Jones, "if we're going to try, the sooner we make a start the better. It will be light enough by the time we reach the caravan."

They all dressed hurriedly. Mrs Jones made steaming hot cups of tea for them to drink before they left, and gave Mr Jones a flask of hot sweet milk for Fluff in case they found her. She also gave him a packet of biscuits. "The child will be hungry," she reminded him.

Willybach, the pampered, was lying on a rug in the kitchen. He could sense the excitement afoot, and must have felt he had something to do with it, for his brown eyes were full of expectation.

They packed themselves and the dog into Mr Jones's van, and a few minutes later they arrived at the caravan. There they found the two stolid policemen unhelpful and obstructive. "Couldn't you wait for Inspector Frost to come back, Miss?"

Leonie had taken charge of the expedition. "No, we can't. Every moment is precious. The scent may be cold even now."

Eventually she cajoled them into letting her take an old jersey of Fluff's.

"Find her, boy!" cried John, after the dog's nose had been buried in the wool. "Find her!" he urged.

Mr Jones spoke quietly to Willybach in Welsh as he attached a long lead to the dog's collar.

Willybach seemed to understand at once what was required of him, and led them to the area round the watering point, circling with his nose close to the ground. It was John who spotted the handkerchief among the trees, where it had fallen from Fluff's pocket when Frisby put her down on her feet.

Willybach took up the scent immediately and set off eagerly up the hill and into the mist. "I reckon I know where he's making for," said Mr Jones after a while. "It's a hut near the edge of the old quarry, one that the shepherds use in the winter time."

They were moving more slowly now. The mist was thick and the path treacherous. Willybach strained all the time at his lead and never faltered.

"It's not far away now," panted Mr Jones. "We'd best go carefully from here on."

"Let's stop here for a few minutes," suggested an equally breathless Leonie, "and plan what to do next."

With Willybach protesting violently, she led them off the path to a level patch of ground. Only a soft, sharp command from Mr Jones kept the dog from barking.

Leonie produced from her pocket a small snub-nosed automatic pistol, and checked the loading. She handled the weapon with a confidence which surprised Mr Jones. "It's all right," she said grimly, "I really do know how to use it."

It was Willybach's threatening growl, and the bristling of his back hairs which first called their attention to the sound of slithering feet on the rocky slopes above.

The growl was sufficient to warn Frisby, and he slewed off into the mist so that all they glimpsed was the dark outline of his body.

"That was Frisby!" shouted John, "I'm sure of it!"

Leonie put the gun back in her pocket and said, almost regretfully, "Well, we shan't be needing this after all."

The sounds of Frisby's movements were soon lost and the little group made ready to move on. Willybach was pulling even harder than before in his eagerness to follow the trail. One frantic surge forward snapped the lead holding him, and he scrambled quickly out of reach, refusing to turn back despite Mr Jones's commands. Whimpering with excitement, he disappeared into the mist.

Standing there on the mountain side, hands on hips, Mr Jones broke into voluble Welsh. It was obvious to the other two that Willybach was being cursed loud and long. It was not until Mr Jones was almost breathless from his outburst that he signalled them to follow the route taken by the dog along the ill-defined path.

The going became even more treacherous and the mist wetter and thicker, as they climbed. Once Leonie slipped, ripping the knee of her slacks and grazing the flesh beneath. John stopped the worst of the bleeding for her with a handkerchief bandage, but the injury slowed down their progress considerably.

Another time they came too close to the edge of the old quarry and had to wait several minutes for Mr Jones to make a careful search for the track they had missed.

At last the hut they were seeking loomed gauntly out of the mist. They moved quickly forward, but paused in surprise as, from within, came the cheerful sound of music. And singing, "Tum ti tum, ti tum tum tum," in time, if not in tune, was Fluff's piping treble.

The door of the hut was slightly ajar. Mr Jones, after one quick look inside, flung it open wide.

Fluff, for whom they had feared the worst, was squatting contentedly among the blankets with one arm round her beloved Willybach's neck, and sharing with him the last of the soft biscuits.

"Hello," she greeted them. And then said darkly to John, "It *was* your turn to fetch the water, you jolly well know it was!"

Chapter Sixteen

The Order that Went Out Too Late

Lunch at the Jones's farm that day was a hilarious affair.

Presiding over the gathering, and serving out large portions of an immense and richly flavoured steak and kidney pie, was a smiling Mrs Jones. Next to her sat Fluff, newly tubbed and scrubbed, with a devoted Willy-bach under her chair. On Fluff's right was Uncle Charles who looked very different from the haggard man of the early hours of the morning.

Then came Leonie. "We'll be two crocks together!" smiled Uncle Charles, as he assisted her to her seat.

At the far end of the table, in charge of the vegetable

dishes, sat Mr Jones. The company was completed by Sergeant Southgate, John and a stoutish army officer in battledress. This was the Brigade Major from the Territorial Army Unit which had been called in to assist with the search.

"If you eat that lot," said John looking at Fluff's heaped plate, "You'll burst!"

"I've got a lot of meals to make up for," replied Fluff with dignity. "It's all very well for some people!"

Major Lowe was recounting how Frisby had broken through the army blocks on the Arthog to Dolgelley road. "My chaps saw this Post Office van with a postman at the wheel – and, of course, no beard – and naturally enough they let him through."

The Major gave a chagrined laugh. "We were just about to move the main body of troops through the roadblocks to start the search, when the real postman came running down the road without his jacket and trousers and with his shirt tails flying in the breeze. He was so gibbering with rage that it took us some time to get him to talk sensibly and tell us what had happened. In fact, if someone hadn't borrowed a pair of trousers for him from a cottage nearby, I think he'd be gibbering yet."

"I suppose Frisby jumped him?" put in Uncle Charles.

"Yes. He had just got out of his van to make a delivery to the house near the waterfall, when Frisby appeared from over the wall and grabbed him. He'd got a nasty-looking rock in his fist and threatened to use it if the postman didn't get out of his clothes sharply enough. Then, when the poor devil was half naked, Frisby tied him up with his braces and dropped him over the wall out of sight."

"How did he get free?"

"That was fairly easy. Frisby hadn't stopped to make a good job of the tying up. But by the time the postman was free, Frisby had changed and was away with the van."

"You know we've found the van and uniform?" remarked Sergeant Southgate.

"Yes, Sergeant," replied Uncle Charles. "The Dolgelley Station Sergeant telephoned just before lunch and told me it had been located, hidden in some trees just outside the town. There's no sign of Frisby anywhere. They've got patrols out on all the roads watching for him to make a break."

"He's not with Evans then, Sir?"

"No, Sergeant. Evans's shop has been thoroughly searched, and although Evans was pulled in for questioning he obviously knows nothing of Frisby's break, and we've had to let him go."

"Can't he be held on suspicion?" queried the Major, who had been informed of the recent happenings.

"No," said Uncle Charles, "unfortunately he can't. We haven't any case against him at all, and he can't be convicted of the same crime twice. It's only if we can prove that he's handled the missing gold that we can touch him. We've no *real* proof of that at the moment. Suspicion isn't proof, unfortunately!"

"Now you must all forget about those nasty people and enjoy your lunch," insisted Mrs Jones. "I will not have the bad taste of their names in your mouths to spoil the flavour of my pie."

Fluff's eyes were slightly glazed by the time she had cleared her plate, despite the fact that from time to time odd bits of meat had been surreptitiously slipped under the table to Willybach.

"T.T.T.T.?" suggested John, sympathetically.

"Yes," murmured the replete Fluff. "Definitely!"

Mrs Jones looked at John with suspicion in her eyes. "And what, pray, does T.T.T.T. stand for?"

John grinned. "Tummy Touching Table Trouble," he explained. "She often gets it. Her eyes are bigger than . . ."

Uncle Charles intervened. "Now, John, remember where you are!"

"Well, it's true, Uncle, you know it is."

Raspberries and cream were being offered round by Mrs Jones. She paused when she came to Fluff. "Well, my dear?"

"Yes please!"

John held his hands in front of his face and protested. "No, no!! Mrs Jones. She'll explode."

"That reminds me," said Uncle Charles, addressing Sergeant Southgate, "did you manage to get the Dolgelley people to put a guard on the old mineshaft. We don't want an explosion there!"

Sergeant Southgate shook his head. "No. Every available man is either out on patrol or manning the road blocks."

"Is there a check-point at Llanelltyd?"

"Yes, but on the Barmouth side of the village."

Uncle Charles shook his head. "That leaves the mine road uncovered. I know it doesn't lead anywhere, but I'm convinced Evans didn't go to all that trouble with empty boxes and explosives without having some purpose in mind."

Leonie intervened: "Something perhaps which Frisby and his sister don't know about. A booby trap of some kind. It would suit Evans's book to have that pair conveniently out of the way."

Major Lowe asked, "Is there anything my chaps can do to help? We've a bunch of Royal Engineers attached to Brigade H.Q., and they can cope with anything in the way of booby traps and explosives. It's just their cup of tea!"

He added ruefully, "I feel we owe you something after this morning's fiasco"

Uncle Charles thanked him. The offer of specialist

help like this was much appreciated. "How quickly can you get some men out there?"

"Right away if you like. All I've got to do is telephone the camp."

"Good." Uncle Charles turned to Sergeant Southgate. "I want you to take your car and meet Major Lowe's men at the road junction in Llanelltyd Village. Go with them up to the mine and see what Evans has been playing at. If there *is* a booby trap, see that it is made harmless."

Major Lowe was already standing by the telephone. "Right. I'll fix it like that."

Having contacted the officer in charge of the detachment of Royal Engineers, he gave a brief explanation of what was happening and a series of brisk orders.

Ten minutes later he and Sergeant Southgate were on their way to Llanelltyd together.

Chapter Seventeen

The Plan that Went Wrong

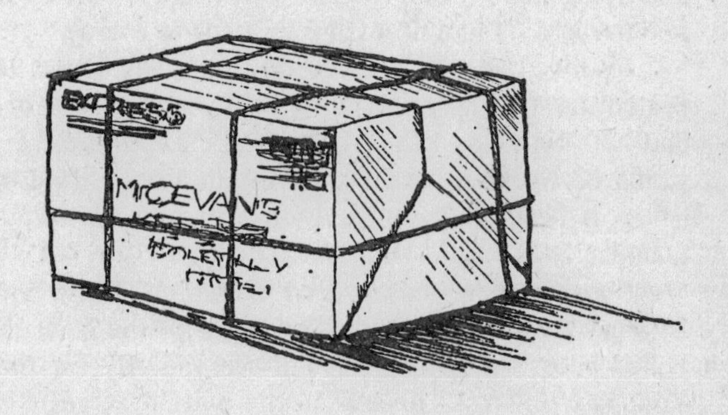

An indignant Evans had been picked up by the police quite early that morning, and questioned at the Station for more than two hours. Meanwhile, his shop, house and outbuildings were thoroughly searched. He denied all present knowledge of Frisby, and swore that he hadn't seen the man since they had faced the judge together in the dock at the Old Bailey.

As for helping him to escape, that was quite impossible. He had been, so he said, with the Chapel choir at the Eisteddfodd on the day of the escape. There were thirty people who could prove it. They would have won the cup that day, if Constable Hughes, who sang the tenor part, hadn't missed his cue with the solo entry. The police, particularly fat policemen, were useless, he remarked. All they could do was hound innocent people for what they didn't know anything about, or for parking their cars for a few minutes where it was convenient and doing nobody any harm. "I can tell you this," he said fiercely. "*I* had no wish for Frisby to escape."

Questioned again about the missing gold, Evans repeated the story that he had told so many times before, and had sworn on oath at the trial. "Do you think I would be working hard, and living in a hole like Dolgelley, if I could lay my hands on a quarter of a million pounds?"

After the report came in that the search of his premises had revealed no sign of Frisby or of the gold, the police had to release him. "I'll see you pay for this, Tommy Williams!" he said to the Station Sergeant as he went out through the door. "Even if you do come to the same chapel!"

Back at the shop, he was just in time to greet the postman who delivered to him a large brown paper parcel which was well secured with thick coarse string. "Express delivery it is, Mr Evans. From London."

And, in all innocence, the representative of Her Majesty's Mails handed over twenty thousand pounds.

Evans thanked him politely, and enquired with concern about the postman's colleague who had been so ill-treated that morning. According to the rumours running around the town, he had lost his trousers to the escaped convict.

"He has them back now, Mr Evans, but he says he will not wear them again after such wickedness. There will have to be another pair supplied by the postmaster."

Evans shook his head sympathetically and picked up his parcel as the postman went on his way. He did not bother to undo the string and check the contents. The exact sum would be there, of that he was sure. Old Crabthorne, the hump-backed, red nosed little stamp dealer, who used his philatelist's shop in Bolson's Cross as a cover for his activities as a fence, was as straight as a die in his undercover dealings!

Nor did he place the parcel in his safe. "Those nosey parker cops are bound to look in there again if they come back," he muttered.

The simplest and easiest way to hide anything was right under everyone's nose, the blindest spot of all! He laughed as he looked round the shop. That was how he had hidden the rest of the gold; just where it stared them all in the face. Frisby had touched some of it, and so had Frost. Yes, Frost had actually laid his hands on some himself and had obviously admired the way in which it was displayed. Evans chuckled. "Clever, clever Mr Frost!"

Then he wrapped up the recently arrived parcel in some of the green and yellow striped paper he used for despatching his overseas orders. He addressed it to a fictitious Elmer P. Zannick in Washington, and placed it among the other parcels waiting collection. "And neither you, Buss Frisby, nor you, Frosty, are likely to bother much with that pile," he muttered, with satisfaction.

A few minutes later, just before one o'clock, a neat black station wagon drew up outside the shop. From it stepped two nuns. With downcast eyes they crossed the pavement and disappeared through the door.

P.C. Hughes, who was still "keeping an eye on things", decided to have a closer look at the station wagon.

Along the panels of the door was neatly printed, ST WINIFRED'S PRIORY. Carefully stacked in the back were six large sacking bundles on which had been stencilled, in bold letters, ST VALMAN'S MISSION STATION, VIA MOMBASA (S.S. KILIMAROH), to which in smaller letters had been added, CLOTHES FOR AFRICA APPEAL (CHEAP RATE). Loose on the floor of the van were several items of discarded clothing.

Remembering that one of the Sisters had been carrying what looked like an almost empty sack, Constable Hughes smiled to himself. "They're not likely to get much out of him this morning!"

Quite satisfied with what he had seen, the Constable moved back to his watching point at the corner of the street.

Inside the shop, Evans turned round to see the black-robed figures advancing upon him like two huge birds of ill omen.

It was Lil Frisby who spoke. Her voice, harsh and uncompromising, belied the peaceful habit she wore. "Got that money?"

Although Evans had fully expected either or both of the Frisbys to contact him during the day, this open call came as a shock. The little man's heart seemed to jump violently in his chest, but he quickly stifled his first feelings of panic. "You fools, you fools, you utter fools!"

"Cut that out!" snarled Frisby.

But Evans was determined to have his say. "You've brought a proper hornet's nest round our ears by touching that kid!"

Frisby's face was contorted with rage. "Shut up! Hand over that money!"

"This is it," thought Evans. "This is where the plan really must begin to work." He whined, "I can't. It hasn't come yet!"

"I told you we'd be a day too soon, Buss," said the woman, in disgust. "We'll just have to settle for what money he's got in the safe, and a load of stuff from the mine."

Towering over Evans, Frisby said, "Gimme the key to the safe."

With calculated reluctance, the little antique dealer felt in his pocket for the key. He held it out for Frisby to take, but then appeared to change his mind. "No! I won't!"

Frisby, in a fit of uncontrollable frenzy, swept up a brass paperweight from the counter and struck Evans down. With a look of anguished surprise, he slumped slowly forward and collapsed in an untidy heap on the floor.

Lil Frisby knelt down quickly beside him and turned him over on to his back. Blood was streaming from an ugly cut on the little man's forehead. He lay still.

"Strewth! You've killed him!"

Frisby took a closer look. "Don't be a fool, Lil. He's out cold, but he's still breathing!"

After that momentary panic, Lil Frisby took control again, just as she had taken control earlier in the day, when her brother had telephoned to say that he was waiting to be picked up outside Dolgelley.

Gathering the voluminous skirts of the nun's habit around her, she moved quickly to the door of the shop and slipped the catch to hold the lock. At the same time she turned the card on the inside of the glass panel so that instead of *OPEN* it read *LUNCH* 1 p.m. to 2 p.m. As she did this, she called out, "Get him behind the counter out of sight!"

Frisby grabbed Evans by the feet and dragged him roughly across the floor.

"Now get the safe open."

The key ring came away easily from Evans's unresisting fingers, and Frisby soon had the safe door swinging back on its hinges. The contents were disappointing. There was about seventy pounds in notes, fifteen poundsworth of silver and a fifty-pence bag of coppers, also a cheque for thirty-five pounds.

Frisby took the notes and stuffed them in the pocket of his robe. Then he turned to the cash register, but it was empty, except for a small float of silver and copper. He cursed aloud.

"O.K!" said his sister. "Let's get going."

"What about him?" Frisby jerked his thumb towards the still figure of Evans.

Lil thought for a moment. "Stuff him in the sack. We'll take him with us and dump him in the mine. Nobody is going to look for him there in a hurry. And by the time he finds his way out we'll be well clear. It's more than his own skin's worth to go to the cops about us anyhow!"

A few minutes later the watching Constable Hughes saw the two nuns leaving the shop. One was dragging a sack, now full and heavy, whilst the other stood by the partly open door obviously saying goodbye, and thanking the little antique dealer for his charity.

"Fancy that now," said the Constable to himself. "That Evans is a queer fish indeed. The next time we have a jumble sale at the chapel I must remember to call on him!"

The nun with the sack had some difficulty in swinging it into the back of the station wagon, and the second nun came to her aid. They seemed to be in no hurry, and before driving off both turned and waved graciously to someone in the shop.

"I suppose I ought to have given them a hand," thought P.C. Hughes, as he watched the vehicle negotiate the corner and head out of the town in the direction of Barmouth.

At Llanelltyd the station wagon turned on to the mine road. Lil, who was driving, stopped just short of the bridge and turned the vehicle round, ready for a quick getaway.

"Come on," she said. "Let's get on with it. The sooner we're loaded the better."

They stripped off their encumbering black robes and flung them into the back of the vehicle. Under the costume both were dressed alike in black slacks and jerseys.

"Lead on," said Frisby. And picking up the limp bundle that was Evans, he flung it across his shoulder and stumbled up the hill after Lil.

"I hope it's not far," he called. "This little perisher weighs more than you'd think to look at him!"

"Come on. Don't waste your breath."

Even the tough Frisby was almost exhausted by the time they reached the side chamber. He dropped his burden with a heavy thud and sat down on a boulder near the opening.

"I've got to have a breather, Lil," he groaned.

"Come on," she snapped, "tip him out here. We'll want that sack for the gold. We can't take the boxes. Somebody might spot 'em."

Frisby muttered under his breath, but did as he was told. Evans's limp body was tumbled out of the bag and lay slumped on the rocky floor face downwards.

Lil Frisby shone her torch on him. "Turn him over. Let's have a look at him."

The bright cone of light played on the tightly closed eyes and pale face of the unconscious man. "Out cold still, Lil."

"Just as well. Leave him. We'll get on with the job."

The pair turned towards the heap of stones in the corner, and began work eagerly.

Evans watched them from under lowered eyelids. He had swum back into a painful awareness of where he was, and what had happened, when he had been tipped out of the bag. He decided it might pay him better to feign unconsciousness until he got his wits about him. His legs and body felt like jelly and his mind was woolly.

But through this pounding haziness he began to realise his danger. "Out, out, out, GET OUT!" his brain insisted. "OUT, OUT, OUT."

Cautiously and unsteadily he got first to his knees and

then, shakily, on to his feet. Lil and her brother were far too busy unpiling stones to hear the scuffling and scrabbling he made.

The boxes were nearly uncovered and Evans's dulled, pain-filled mind told him he was only seconds away from death. Stumbling forward, he broke into a shambling run and was well clear of the side shaft and into the main tunnel before Lil Frisby, with a feeling that all was not well, turned her torch to where he had been lying.

"Buss!" she screamed. "After him! The little perisher's got away!"

Buss, the uppermost of the boxes already in his hands, slewed partly round. As he did so a spring clicked neatly into place. Current, from the torch battery in the box he held, flashed through to the detonators buried in the hidden gelignite. There was a momentary blue-white glare, then a roar of explosion as a great section of the tunnel roof collapsed.

Evans was clear of the fall, but the fierce blast from the explosion threw him down on his face. Choking with the swirling smoke and dust, his eardrums pounding from the noise, he began to crawl on his hands and knees to safety. Only determination to live drove him on. His plan had worked.

Although he was only barely conscious, he was still aware of a feeling of exultation. He would be troubled no more by Frisby and his grasping sister; and all the gold was *his*. This was only right for it *was* his gold and he had worked hard to get it. The Frisbys would stay trapped in the chamber for all time, with only boxes full of rubbish to keep them company.

He was still cackling with hysterical laughter when he reeled out of the mouth of the shaft and into the bright light of day.

For a moment he blinked with red-rimmed eyes at the sky and the hills and the white blobs of distant sheep. Then, as he saw some figures in khaki uniforms running up from the bridge towards him, his knees suddenly gave way and he collapsed and fell forward in a state of complete unconsciousness.

Sergeant Southgate and Major Lowe were the first to reach him. They had arrived at the bridge with a party of Royal Engineers only a few minutes before the explosion. It was whilst they had been examining the station wagon, and puzzling over the discarded robes, that the ground beneath their feet had shivered with the shock wave, and a cloud of smoke and dust had suddenly erupted from the entrance to the mine-shaft.

"Who the . . . ?" spluttered Major Lowe, as the young Police Sergeant gently turned Evans over on to his back and felt for his pulse. The little man's face was white and haggard beneath the grime and encrusted blood.

"It's Evans!" he announced. "He's still alive but in pretty bad shape, I think."

"Do you think anyone else is down there?" asked the Major, peering at the dust still swirling at the mine-shaft entrance.

"Goodness only knows! But my guess is that Frisby and his sister are both in there."

Major Lowe stood up and pushed his service cap to the back of his balding pate. "If they are," he said, "the chances of getting them out alive are a bit dicey. That was a heck of a bang!"

Major Lowe called to the Corporal in charge of the army detachment. "We'll have a quick look and see what's happened. Meanwhile, Southgate, I'd better get one of my chaps to go back and phone for a doctor."

"Yes," agreed Sergeant Southgate. "And at the same time he can contact Inspector Frost for me. I don't think my Chief is going to be too pleased about all this!"

Chapter Eighteen

Rescue Operations

It was the second occasion within a very short time that Inspector Frost had peered anxiously at his watch. Sergeant Southgate, who was squatting by the field telephone at the entrance to the mine, realised that his chief was getting really worried.

The local Superintendent of Police who stood with Inspector Frost did not seem in the least perturbed, however. "This could be a long job, Inspector," he remarked. "But there is nothing more we can do now those two mine rescue experts have joined up with the army team. We've just got to leave it to them."

Several hours had elapsed since the explosion and the

dramatic appearance of Evans out of the smoke and dust. That member of the crooked trio now lay, unconscious, in the local hospital, under strict police guard.

It was the whereabouts of the other two, Frisby and his sister, which was worrying Inspector Frost. Were they in the mine? Or weren't they? And if they were there, were they alive or were they dead?

Sergeant Southgate's report that there had been an explosion at the mine had set many wheels in motion. Rescue operations were started in the mine, and, just in case Frisby and his sister had escaped, police patrols were intensified and extended.

"I suppose if those two are in there, and still alive, we'd better do our best to get 'em out," Uncle Charles had said, and added gloomily, "but what good that'll do the community I don't know."

So it was that Major Lowe's team, with the two mine rescue experts, were now hard at work removing fallen rock and shoring up the tunnel against further falls as they burrowed deeper into the earth.

The local Police Superintendent had driven over to the mine accompanied by a sheepish Constable Hughes. "Here you are, Frost. This is Constable Hughes. If you want to question him go ahead."

Hughes was terribly upset. "Right under my nose, Sir," he said angrily, "those two nuns walked into that shop and out again without my suspecting a thing. Not a thing!"

"What about Evans?"

"He must have been in that bag, Inspector. He didn't come out on his own two feet, I will swear to that."

Uncle Charles gave the man a curt nod of dismissal,

and strolled down towards the bridge where Fluff, John and Miss Bretherton had been caught up in a knot of journalists and a television crew.

"It's worse than being a film star," grumbled John. "I don't know how I'll ever live it down at school. As for you, Fluff, anyone who believes all that sob story rot needs his head examined!"

"I can't help what they put in the papers, can I?" retorted Fluff.

"Well, it's going a bit far when the wireless chap says" – and here John mimicked the announcer who had given the lunchtime news – *"and Andrew James, our man on the spot at Dolgelley, now gives an account of the child's night of terror in the mountain hut."*

Fluff chuckled. "You're only jealous!"

"Night of terror, my foot! There you were, feeding your face, sleeping like a log and getting presents of transistor sets, and all the time we were worrying ourselves sick!" John appealed to Leonie. "She should have seen Uncle Charles, shouldn't she, Miss Bretherton? He was frantic!"

Leonie, smilingly, shook her head. "I think we all were," she replied. "None of us dreamed you'd tame that savage beast, Fluff. Here comes your Uncle now. Let's ask him what's happening."

But the newspaper men had already closed round the Inspector to question him themselves. Leonie, Fluff and John, at Fluff's suggestion, made instead for an ice-cream van which, taking advantage of the situation, had arrived on the spot to do a roaring trade with the small crowd which had so quickly gathered to watch proceedings.

"I'll stand you a sixpenny cone if you get them, John," Fluff volunteered in the generous manner of all heroines. "And get one for Miss Bretherton too. After all, I do owe you both something for rescuing me – even if I didn't need rescuing."

"Fiona Carr, you're a horror!" exclaimed Leonie, "you surely can't want ice cream after all that lunch. You will explode!"

But the ice creams were forgotten when things began to happen at the mineshaft.

Sergeant Southgate, who had been buzzed on the telephone by Major Lowe who was in the mine, was signalling urgently for Uncle Charles to return.

He held up two fingers for all to see. "It looks as though they've got the two of them," observed John, interpreting the sign.

Inspector Frost hurried back up the hill, his limp more noticeable than ever after his tiring night and day of effort.

"I'll give you a story," he called back over his shoulder to the clamouring reporters, "as soon as I know what's happened."

Sergeant Southgate had already handed over the telephone to the Police Superintendent. He quickly put Uncle Charles in the picture.

"They heard some tapping a couple of minutes ago, and then some faint shouting. It's Frisby all right, and, as far as they can make out, they are both safe."

The Superintendent put the telephone down and joined them.

"How much further have they got to go to reach Frisby and his sister?" the Inspector asked.

"They think there's only another ten to fifteen feet of fall," said the Superintendent, "but they are having to go carefully now. The rocks above are so badly disturbed that they are having to shore up every foot of the way. If the extra load of timbers we've asked for doesn't arrive soon, work will have to stop."

"We'd better get an ambulance and doctor to stand by anyway," said Uncle Charles. "And we can call off our patrols and road blocks."

It was almost nine o'clock in the evening before the rescue operations were completed.

Fluff and John had pleaded earnestly with their Uncle Charles to be allowed to stay on to watch, and Leonie had supported them. "I'll look after them, Inspector, and take them off for a meal when they get hungry," she offered. "And while we are away in the town, I'll phone Mrs Jones and tell her what's happening and that we shall be late back."

During lunch it had been arranged that both Fluff and John should sleep at the farm that night, and Fluff, who had been shown the little room she was to have, with its pink rosebud wallpaper and neat white bed, was thrilled with the idea. Willybach would not be far away and she had a feeling that it might not be impossible to persuade Mrs Jones to let him sleep in her room.

So Uncle Charles allowed them to stay on until Frisby and his sister were brought to the surface.

Excitement among the reporters and the watching crowd began to run high when increased activity at the opening to the mine indicated that the moment of release was nearing.

The doctor, who had been down the mine for some time, emerged to signal to the ambulance driver that he and his mate should bring a stretcher. Two sturdy Police Constables from a patrol car followed the ambulance men up the hill. One had a set of handcuffs dangling significantly from his wrist in readiness for an arrest.

Frisby was the first out. He was on his two feet but had his left arm in a sling. His sister, suffering from loss of blood owing to a bad gash in her scalp, and dazed with shock, had to be carried out on the stretcher.

Nothing much could be seen of her beneath the blankets and the white swathe of bandage that covered her head.

There had been no word of thanks from Frisby as he stumbled by the tired men who had rescued them, but he pulled up sharply in front of Inspector Frost, his eyes dark with rage. "Have you got him?"

Uncle Charles nodded. There was no need to ask whom Frisby meant.

"Alive?"

"Yes."

Frisby spat, but said no more. His face however, clearly showed his intention of finding Evans one day and choking the life out of him. Fluff shivered as he passed by her.

Leonie put her arm round Fluff's shoulder and gave her an affectionate squeeze. "It's all right now, my dear."

"Yes!" said Uncle Charles, as he joined them. "I don't think Frisby will get away again in a hurry."

They watched as he was bundled into a police car amid a battery of press cameras, and saw the car disappear from sight down the hill closely followed by the ambulance.

"And now to bed, you two!" ordered Uncle Charles. "Sleep well, I'll see you all in the morning."

John asked, "Are you going to have another hunt for the gold tomorrow?"

"Yes. You can come and join the search if you like."

Leonie said: "I suppose nothing's been heard from Evans?"

"No. He was still in a coma when the last report came in from the hospital an hour ago. There may even be a possibility of brain damage."

"You mean he may never talk?"

"Yes, that's possible."

Leonie looked despondent.

"In that case," she remarked, "I don't see how we will ever find the rest of the bullion."

Uncle Charles was much more optimistic. "I think we will. You'll see!"

"How?"

Uncle Charles laughed. "We'll put Fluff and Willy-bach on the job and give the dog a sniff at a golden sovereign before they start."

Even Leonie smiled at that suggestion.

Then Uncle Charles firmly led them off to Leonie's car. "In you get, and on your way. I still have one or two more things to attend to here then I'm for bed myself."

He watched as they moved off down the road, and then made his way slowly back up the hill to where Major Lowe, the rescue experts and the detachment of soldiers had gathered. They had done a grand job of work and someone should thank them for it.

Chapter Nineteen

Fluff Makes Up Her Mind

The next morning Fluff woke surprisingly early. She was awake, in fact, at six o'clock when Mr Jones gently opened the door of her room and softly whistled for Willybach to join him.

"Hello Mr Jones," said Fluff, to the farmer's surprise. "Can I come too?"

"You'd better stay where you are, young lady. If you don't, we'll have Mrs Jones after us, and we'll all be in trouble!"

Fluff chortled wickedly under the blankets. "We wouldn't want that, would we, Mr Jones? All right, I'll stay here, but you won't keep Willybach away too long will you? Promise?"

"No, we shan't be long. Mrs Jones always gets breakfast ready for eight o'clock and we'll be back for that, won't we boy?"

Willybach looked up at his master, and it seemed to Fluff as though he was smiling his agreement. He pushed his nose into Fluff's hand in a goodbye gesture and followed his master from the room.

When they had gone, and the door was shut again, Fluff propped herself up in bed with her pillows so that she could look out across the fields to where the rising sun flared through a group of trees on a hillside crest.

She thought about the happenings of the previous day and of the evening when, very tired and sleepy, she and John had been given hot milky drinks in the kitchen and sent off to bed.

She had not even had the energy to persuade Mrs Jones to let Willybach sleep in her room. Willybach and Mrs Jones themselves suggested it. "He'll be company for you, dear," she said, as the dog rose at Fluff's heels.

So the dog had slept on a rug by her bed, and she fell asleep with one hand buried deeply in his hair.

"Oh, dear," she thought, "what's going to happen now? What happens after today?" She had already sounded Uncle Charles out on the subject of Willybach during one of the long spells of waiting by the mine-shaft entrance.

"How much do you think Willybach is really worth?" she had asked.

"Quite a lot I should imagine, Fluff."

"But how much?" she persisted.

Uncle Charles had considered the matter carefully.

"Perhaps twenty-five or thirty pounds. It would be even more if he were a fully trained dog like Ben and Sheila."

Ben and Sheila were Mr Jones's other dogs. They really had Welsh names but Ben and Sheila seemed the only pronouncable equivalents, and so Ben and Sheila they became.

"Oh!" said Fluff in horror. "That *is* a lot."

For the moment she had let the matter drop. Now she doubled up her knees in bed, resting her chin on the heaped pile of bedclothes, and stared out at the sunrise.

She then went into what she called 'one of her big thinks'.

"Let's suppose Mr Jones could see his way to selling Willybach to me for twenty-five pounds." That was the smallest sum Uncle Charles had suggested. "How can I possibly raise twenty-five pounds?" she murmured. Reckoning up everything she possessed, including the ninety pence John owed her, and even allowing for the week's pocket money which was due on Saturday, it still came to no more than six pounds and seventy-one pence.

"I wonder if John would buy the tranny Frisby gave me," she mused. "That must be worth quite a lot. It's a good one. He ought to give me five pounds for it, that is, if he wants it enough, and if he's got five pounds!"

"Would Uncle Charles lend me the rest?" Anyone looking in the room at that moment would have seen her shaking her dark, curly head in a gesture of solemn resignation. "No, he wouldn't."

It wasn't as though he was mean. He wasn't. That was the last thing you could ever say about Uncle

Charles. He was a dear, but he had told her once before, when she had wanted desperately to buy something, "Save up for it. Don't ever get into debt, my dear, it just isn't worth it." Then he had helped her to save the money by finding jobs for her to do which seemed to attract generous rewards.

"No, I just can't ask him. Besides . . . " Two big tears gathered and began to roll down her cheeks. "Besides we couldn't keep Willybach in a flat in London. It wouldn't be fair to him, for he loves the countryside and the hills. It would be downright rotten for him!"

There was school, too. Dogs weren't allowed at boarding school, and she wouldn't see Willybach for weeks and weeks and weeks. Uncle Charles would be kind to him, of course, while she was away, but it wouldn't be the same.

She looked through tear-misted eyes to the hillside where Mr Jones stood with his three dogs.

Willybach was easy to recognise. At Mr Jones's whistled command, he scampered gladly off to gather in a ewe and lamb from the corner of the field.

She heard, very faintly, his short sharp bark.

"No!" she said firmly to herself. "I won't try to buy him. He's much happier here. It just won't do! Even if I never see him again."

Chapter Twenty

The Gold that did not Glister

Fluff was unusually quiet at breakfast. Occasionally she glanced wistfully down at Willybach, who waited by her chair in patient expectation of scraps, and once or twice there was a hint of a sigh.

Leonie, who sat opposite, guessed what was passing through Fluff's mind. She had noticed the signs of tears when she had gone to call Fluff for breakfast. It was a problem which Leonie knew she could not solve and so, to distract Fluff's attention, she turned the talk to the matter of the missing gold. "Are you two coming with me to help with the search, or would you both rather go swimming?"

John and Fluff were quick with their replies. There would be other chances for swimming but it was quite unlikely they would ever get another opportunity to take part in a real treasure hunt.

"We're going to help you to look!" cried John, "Aren't we, Fluff?"

"We jolly well are. We can go swimming any time after we've found the gold."

Mr and Mrs Jones joined with Leonie in laughter at Fluff's confident and emphatic answer.

Fluff became indignant, and added, "Of course we are going to find it. At least Uncle Charles is. He's much more clever than silly old Evans. Ten times more clever, in fact."

This brought more laughter, and Fluff suddenly realised that everyone was looking over her shoulder to the door leading from the back kitchen. She turned in her chair. There, framed in the doorway, stood a smiling Uncle Charles. In the background, grinning widely, was Sergeant Southgate.

"Thank you, Fluff, for that vote of confidence. I can only hope you are right."

The newcomers had both breakfasted; Sergeant Southgate at his hotel, and Uncle Charles at Police Superintendent Taylor's home where he had stayed overnight. But they both accepted the cups of tea which Mrs Jones insisted on pouring out for them.

Uncle Charles, who looked much better for a good night's sleep, told them the latest news of Evans and how the big treasure hunt was being planned for the day.

As far as Evans himself was concerned, the news was

disappointing. The hospital now reported that he had recovered consciousness and was out of danger, but he had completely lost his memory. "He doesn't know who he is, where he is, or how he got there."

"Will this loss of memory last for long?" asked Leonie anxiously. She had hoped that Evans might have broken down under persistent questioning, and given a clue to the gold's whereabouts. This development meant that questioning would be useless at present.

Uncle Charles shook his head. "The doctor in charge of the case says he just doesn't know. He's certain it's a genuine case of amnesia, and it could go on for days or weeks or years!"

"Or forever," added Sergeant Southgate, lugubriously.

"Or forever, as you so happily put it," said Uncle Charles. "And that means, young man, that we had better get on with the search, and expect no help with it from Mr Caradoc – confound him – Evans."

Uncle Charles then quickly outlined his plans. Sergeant Southgate was to take charge of operations at Caffryn Mawr, and the antique shop at Dolgelley would have the personal attention of Uncle Charles himself. "I don't for one moment think you are likely to have much luck at your end, Southgate, but we must give the farm a good going over. Evans would never have sold the place to Mr Jones if the gold was still there, you can be sure of that, but I still think we ought to give some attention to the area of the old cottage and the burial chamber by Druid's Oaks."

For this task the Sergeant was to be given three policemen and six of Major Lowe's men, who were now standing by, equipped with mine detectors and ready for action. The balance of the men available, six Constables and two soldiers, would assist Uncle Charles in Dolgelley.

Fluff was puzzled by the mention of mine detectors. "It's gold we're looking for, isn't it?" she whispered to John. "Not more explosives! What are mine detectors, anyway?"

John explained graphically. "Like a kind of broom. You push them along in front of you. They've got earphones attached, and if you get near metal they make a noise, and if it's a mine you have to go jolly carefully or you could blow yourself up."

Mr Jones had been following Uncle Charles's conversation with close interest. "Try those sound things on the walls then, Sergeant," he suggested. "You could hide a lot in those stone walls near the burial chamber. Some are four feet thick and more in parts."

"That's certainly worth trying," said Uncle Charles. "Make sure you examine the walls of the old cottage, too, Sergeant. Evans is fly enough to realise that a short move from the floor to the walls would be just as deceptive, and a lot easier than moving the gold three or four miles."

Leonie said that she wanted to have a quick look round the farm buildings first, and then she would join Uncle Charles's search party in Dolgelley.

"And we are coming too," announced Fluff. "So don't you find it before we get there, Uncle."

With that instruction, Uncle Charles and Sergeant Southgate departed and went to pick up their assistants, leaving Fluff and Company to finish breakfast.

About three quarters of an hour later, Leonie drove her mini car up to Caffryn Mawr with Fluff and John as passengers.

The search there was already in full swing, with the troops and their mine detectors carefully covering the hillside and surrounding walls, and Sergeant Southgate and his policemen at work in the farmhouse itself.

The Sergeant took them upstairs to the room that Frisby had used when he had been hiding at the farmhouse. It showed signs of his occupation, with numerous cigarette ends lying in the fireplace and some empty tins in the corner.

"You know, Fluff," announced John looking out of the window, "if I had shinned up that drainpipe the first night we were here, I should have seen all this and I might even have seen Frisby."

"It's probably just as well you didn't," said Sergeant Southgate. "Frisby's a nasty piece of work, and how Fluff came to no harm with him is something we still don't understand. He even asked the Inspector last night if you were all right, Fluff!"

Apparently Frisby had been in a talkative mood the previous evening. This talk had mainly consisted of threats against Evans, but much had been learned about the escape from Dartmoor in the nuns' outfits, and of the visit to Evans's shop.

Frisby had said, "He was proper scared, too, when Lil and I walked in on him. Fair shook up he was. He knew I was on the run, mind you, but he didn't reckon on Lil getting me through that easy. The little perisher couldn't get me out of the shop fast enough and had me up at that stinking farm the next day. He'd still got a key to the place even though it had changed hands."

Then he added with feeling, "Cor, it was creepy too up there in the dark, and me on me Jack Jones."

Leonie asked Sergeant Southgate if Frisby had mentioned looking for the gold himself.

"Oh yes. He said he had looked for it both at the shop and up here. The only traces of it he found were in the outhouse where the big black cauldron is suspended. From among the ashes under the cauldron he raked out several lead seals like those you found, and also some bits of charred wood which could have come from the bullion boxes. He reckons Evans may have melted down some of the gold when he was living here and sold it to buy the shop in Dolgelley."

"Frisby could be right. That shop would have cost more to set up than he got from Mr Jones for the farm."

Sergeant Southgate added, "Frisby's opinion, for what it's worth, is that the bulk of the gold is still at the shop. He knows Evans has sold some recently because he was supposed to be getting twenty thousand pounds for his South American trip. That was due to arrive at the shop either yesterday or today, in used pound notes and dollar bills, but how it was to be sent Frisby didn't know. He doesn't seem to care about the gold any more. All he wants to do is get his hands on Evans."

"Well," said Leonie, making for the stairway, "I'm of the same opinion as Frisby, so the sooner we get down there and help with the search the sooner we are likely to find it. Come on you two! Goodbye and good luck to you, Sergeant!"

The red mini came to an abrupt halt at the junction with the Arthog Road into Dolgelley. The main road was solidly packed with cars trying to get in or through the town, and their drivers were in varying stages of horn-blowing frustration.

"What on earth . . .?" Leonie exclaimed, and then realised what was happening.

The newspaper and television accounts of the dramatic events of the previous day had brought hordes of sightseers to Dolgelley. And chaos reigned in the town's narrow streets.

"Let's leave your car on the verge here, Miss Bretherton, and see if we can get through on foot," suggested John after they had waited several minutes without seeing any sign of movement in the main stream of traffic. "It isn't all that far to walk."

Leonie agreed. "I think we had better do that, otherwise we shall be here all day."

It was a wise decision, as they soon found when they reached the centre of the town and saw how many people were crowding the pavements and overflowing into the roads. They had considerable difficulty in reaching the shop, particularly after Fluff was recognised and people began to close in on them in rather a frightening way.

"That's her!"

"That's the kid who nearly got killed!"

Thousands of eyes seemed to be peering down at Fluff as they pushed and elbowed their way through to the barriers which had been erected around the antique shop to prevent its windows from being pushed inwards.

Inside this protective enclosure Uncle Charles and Superintendent Taylor were dealing with the eager questions of the twenty or so journalists who had been allowed to join them.

"Give us a break, chaps!" appealed Uncle Charles holding up his hand in protest. "We'll give you the story when there's one to give, but just for the moment there's a lot to be done. The Super's got to get this traffic sorted out, and I've work to do inside."

It was Superintendent Taylor who first spotted the dishevelled Leonie, the somewhat angry John and the rather overwhelmed Fluff standing by the barrier, and he instructed the Constable on watch to let them through.

"Phew!" exclaimed Fluff. "What a relief."

Then she glared at the two photographers who came forward with their cameras at the ready. "No more pictures, please! There have been more than enough already."

But shutters clicked as Uncle Charles led them off into the peaceful haven of the shop's interior. "That, my dear Fluff, is the penalty of fame," pronounced her Uncle, "as all the pop stars discover to their cost!"

They were met inside by a jubilant Constable Hughes. He held out a partly unwrapped parcel for the Inspector to see. "It's the money, Sir!" he cried out with glee. And, placing the parcel on the counter, he began pulling out wad after wad of notes.

"How did you come across that, Hughes?"

"It was on the floor with the other parcels that Evans had made up to send away. I checked them against the despatch book, but this one wasn't recorded; so I opened it up, Sir."

"Well done, man!"

Constable Hughes visibly swelled with pride. He felt now that he had made up for his failure of the previous day, when the Frisbys had kidnapped Evans from under his nose.

A clerk from a nearby bank was called in to check the notes, and the search in the shop and outhouses was continued with new hope.

The Constables were at work in the shop, methodically checking the brassware on every shelf, and the two soldiers were in the cellar testing the floor and walls with their mine detectors. John went to join them.

Uncle Charles turned to Leonie. "Any ideas, Miss Bretherton? After all, it's your gold!"

Leonie corrected him. "My company's gold, since they paid out the insurance on it. As to ideas, the answer is no. I expect, though, it's staring us right in the face."

"That's what I felt the day we were here with Evans. That rascal was laughing at me and enjoying the joke." Uncle Charles paused, then said suddenly, "I wonder!"

He moved quickly to the stairway that led up to the balcony, opened his penknife and began scraping the black paint away from the scrollwork supporting the handrail. It was wrought iron underneath.

But when he scraped a sliver of paint from one of the cast figures of the women in Welsh costume, a streak of bright yellow appeared. The figure had been cast in gold and blackened to look like iron.

"I've got it!" he yelled, in a most un-Inspectorlike manner.

John and the soldiers rushed up from the cellar. The policemen put down the brassware they had been looking at, and everyone crowded round Uncle Charles as he scraped away another patch of paint.

It was a wonderful moment. Fluff and John, joined by a laughing Leonie, did a triumphant dance in the middle of the floor. If Uncle Charles hadn't also been Chief Inspector Frost he would undoubtedly have taken part as well.

As it was, he called off the search and set everyone to work unbolting the figures from the stair, gallery and alcove railings. There were forty-five figures in all. Three were found to be of iron, the rest were gold.

Superintendent Taylor, recalled hurriedly from the Police Station, examined one of the iron ladies with interest. "Evans must have been replacing the gold figures as he converted each one into cash. I think I'll keep this one as an official souvenir of the case."

When all the gold had been neatly stacked and made ready for transfer to the vaults of the local bank, Uncle Charles allowed the Press and Television cameramen into the shop to take pictures.

"There you are, gentlemen. There it is. That's what we've been looking for. Half a ton of gold and, at today's prices, worth nearly a quarter of a million pounds!"

"Is there any missing, Inspector?" asked a reporter.

"Some, of course, but Evans has only been getting rid of it slowly I should think. He'd get a better price from whoever was handling it for him by going warily."

"Will you be able to trace the fence?"

"I doubt it. The parcel of notes, which has also been found, just bears a London postmark. It contains nothing worth following up in the way of a clue. Some of the money could be from the big mail train robbery, but nearly half of it was in American dollar bills."

By lunch time the golden ladies were all safely stowed away in a Dolgelley bank, and the bank was being kept under special watch by Constable Hughes and a fellow policeman.

"And there mustn't be any mistakes this time, Hughes," instructed Superintendent Taylor. "Anything suspicious must be reported to the Station immediately. There will be no peace of mind for any of us until Dolgelley's rid of that troublesome stuff."

The big search was over and all that remained now was to tidy up the loose ends of the case, and of course write the official reports.

Uncle Charles thought of these and groaned inwardly. He picked up the telephone in what had been

Evans's living-room and put in a priority call to Scotland Yard.

While he was doing this, Fluff went out to the workshop and retrieved her brass matchbox dragon. After all, Evans had *given* it to her.

John went with her. "It doesn't shine very much," he remarked, looking at it with disdain, "but I suppose it will do. After all, we found some gold this morning and that didn't glister, did it?"

Chapter Twenty-One

The Happy Re-union

Sunday was a sad day when with a shower of tears from Fluff, they said goodbye to all their new friends in the cosy kitchen at the Jones's farmhouse. Leonie, who had been given the responsibility of supervising the transfer of the gold to London, was staying on at the farm for a few days, but Sergeant Southgate had left for Scotland Yard earlier that morning.

Willybach sensed what was about to happen and he, too, was unhappy, slinking around with his tail down and a look in his liquid brown eyes as though he had been soundly beaten.

"I think Willybach would cry too, if he could," said Mrs Jones, putting an arm round Fluff in an effort to comfort her. "Look at his face!"

The return journey to London was a silent one, after some early attempts by Uncle Charles and John to lighten the gloom. Fluff huddled herself up on the back seat, amid a stack of bottled preserves and home-made pickles pressed upon them from Mrs Jones's store cupboard, and just stared with unseeing eyes through the window.

"Leave her alone," murmured Uncle Charles to John, after a brotherly crack had brought a tearful rejoinder. "She'll get over it in a while."

Back in London, with the weather as wretched as it could be, Uncle Charles, assisted on several occasions by Leonie, now a frequent visitor to the flat, organised all kinds of trips and theatre parties in an effort to cheer up the disconsolate Fluff.

One day they went to the London Planetarium in Baker Street, where they saw a wonderful display of the stars in their courses. Then afterwards, Uncle Charles took his party into Madame Tussaud's next door, and led the way into the gloomy Chamber of Horrors. There the kindly Uncle Charles became Chief Detective Inspector Frost again, and introduced them to the wax effigy of a man he had arrested, and who was later hanged for a murder he had committed in a Brixton public house.

His companions stood puzzled before the pale figure with its staring close-set eyes.

"He was guilty of four murders altogether, although we could only pin this one on him."

"But, Charles," exclaimed Leonie, "isn't that . . . ?"

"It's Frisby!" said Fluff and John together.

"No," smiled Uncle Charles, "it isn't. He was Frisby's

cousin. They're a bad lot in this particular branch of the Frisby clan. In addition to Buss and his sister Lil, and this chap of course, there are two uncles we've had trouble with, and three Frisby cousins who are out-and-out villains."

"Well Buss won't worry anyone for a while," commented Leonie. "And if his sister loses her leg because of the explosion, which seems possible, that will keep her quiet too."

Best of all Fluff enjoyed her visits to London Zoo. On several occasions, when Uncle Charles and Leonie disappeared for mysterious trips into the country, she was allowed to make the long but easy bus journey across to Regents Park from Kensington. There she spent many happy hours among the animals she loved so much.

It was the smaller and lesser known creatures that most appealed to her: those which her favourite author, Gerald Durrell, wrote about in his *Overloaded Ark*, *The New Noah*, and the hilariously funny *Bafut Beagles.*

She also had a specially soft spot for the otters after spending a rapturous two days deeply engrossed in a lovely book, given her by Leonie, called *A Ring of Bright Water*. It recounted the experiences of the author when he shared his home with, and gained the trust and friendship of, an otter. "One day," she promised herself as she finished the book, "I would like a home in the country where I could make friends with the wild animals and perhaps even find an otter willing to be friends with me."

It was about three weeks after their return to London

that Uncle Charles announced at breakfast, "We are all going to dinner at the Hilton tonight."

Both Fluff and John knew of this modern hotel in Park Lane, with its tower soaring high into the sky way above the treetops of Hyde Park.

"Who do you mean by *all*, Uncle?" asked Fluff.

"The Insurance Company is giving a party to celebrate the recovery of the gold," explained her uncle. "There will be people there from the company, someone from Scotland Yard, and us." He added, "Leonie will be arriving soon, Fluff, to take you shopping. You'll need a nice new dress."

It was a splendid shopping spree which occupied all morning. They chose a neat little red dress with a discreet pattern. There were new black shoes too, very different from the strapped or laced ones that Fluff normally wore at school, and Leonie insisted that she had a matching handbag.

"This is going to be a very special occasion, Fluff, and tonight you and I are going to look our very best."

Normally the family travelled around London by bus or tube, but the trip to the hotel that evening was a special one, and made by taxi.

Uncle Charles was resplendent in a dinner jacket from which, thought Fluff, there came the slightest suspicion of a smell of moth balls. Following a last minute decision John had been rushed into a new dark suit and was feeling rather self conscious.

"Your carriage awaits, Madam," John called, as he opened the taxi door and gave an exaggerated bow to Fluff standing in the entrance hall to their block of flats.

Miss Fiona Carr's descent of the steps in her full finery would have been impressive if she had not stubbed her toe on a paving stone and nearly tumbled over.

"Drat it!" she exclaimed and hopped into the taxi to flop down beside her laughing uncle and nurse her foot.

Leonie, very lovely in an emerald green chiffon dress which set off her flaming, and, for once, tidy hair, was waiting to greet them in the hotel lounge. "You look very nice," she complimented Fluff.

"And you look beautiful, doesn't she, Uncle?"

"It's a pleasure to be with both of you," replied Uncle Charles tactfully.

They were then led to a private room where two gentlemen, of most distinguished appearance stood together with cocktail glasses in hand.

Introductions were made. One of the gentlemen was the Assistant Commissioner at Scotland Yard who had written to Uncle Charles asking him to take charge of the Dolgelley investigations.

"Good evening, Frost," he said, coming across to shake his hand warmly. "Well done!"

The other gentleman was introduced as Sir Jonas Brownrigg, the Chairman of the Insurance Company.

He seemed to be especially interested in Fluff. "So you are the young woman the papers made so much fuss about? You don't look as though you were particularly badly treated."

"I don't think I was," admitted Fluff. "I can't say I enjoyed it and I was a bit frightened at first, but now it's all over, I wouldn't have missed it for worlds."

John was wondering about the table in the room which was set for eight persons. Two guests were still missing according to his reckoning, and he was about to ask Leonie who was expected when Sir Jonas held up his hand and called for silence.

"For a very special reason I want to make some presentations before our other guests arrive."

He produced from his inner pocket two envelopes. "The first of these is for you, Inspector Frost, for your part in the recovery of the gold. As you are aware, my company offered a substantial reward, and the police authorities have agreed, because of the special circumstances in your case, that part of this reward could be paid to you. So, Inspector Frost, on behalf of my Board of Directors, and with their grateful thanks for all you have done, it gives me great pleasure to hand you this cheque for £5,000."

The Assistant Commissioner said, with a smile, "Not bad for a week's work, Frost! Even if you did have a fair whack of report writing at the end of it!"

Sir Jonas next turned to Leonie. "In this envelope, my dear, is another cheque for £5,000. This is for you, and again I bring from my board an expression of their warmest appreciation for your work."

He paused, and then went on, "To neither you, Inspector, nor you, Miss Bretherton, do these presentations come as a complete surprise, and I hear the money has already been earmarked for a property investment in the country . . ."

Fluff and John, both hopelessly bewildered by this remark, looked first at Leonie and then at Uncle Charles, and were just bursting to ask questions, when

Sir Jonas continued, "... And so, to you both, my own personal congratulations, and sincere good wishes for your happy future together."

There was a moment of confusion, with Sir Jonas and the Assistant Commissioner smiling, Uncle Charles looking, of all things, rather shy, and Leonie blushing as if to compete with her flaming hair.

Then Uncle Charles took Leonie's left hand and held it out so that John and Fluff could see the pretty engagement ring.

"We're g-going to g-get m-married," he stuttered, "and ... "

But Leonie took over. "And we've bought a house in the country quite close to your school, so that you can live at home instead of being boarders ... "

Here Leonie signalled a waiter to open the door. "And so that Willybach can come to live with us too."

In walked a laughing Mr and Mrs Jones, and in rushed Willybach, his coat sleek and shining with much brushing.

An uproarious ten minutes followed. Fluff wildly hugged and kissed in turn, Willybach, Uncle Charles, Leonie, Mr and Mrs Jones, the smiling Sir Jonas and even the astonished, but nevertheless delighted, Assistant Commissioner.

John solemnly shook hands with everyone, not knowing what else to do, and slightly embarrassed by his sister's exuberance. Then Leonie handed him a small square parcel labelled "Especially for John". Inside was the 35 mm. camera he had long wanted to own, together with films and flash equipment.

"Gosh!" he exclaimed, and, forgetting his views on

sloppy behaviour, hugged her warmly. "Thanks! Oh thank you! This is just the thing."

With the aid of the Assistant Commissioner, who was another camera enthusiast, he set to work taking pictures of the occasion. The best one he got was of Fluff sitting on the floor with an arm around Willybach, a glass of champagne in her hand, and tears of joy streaming down her face.

"I can't help it," she was saying. "I don't want to cry, but I'm so happy. I've just got to!" Willybach responded by licking her face.

The party was over, and Fluff back at the flat where Leonie had tucked her up in bed. Under the bed lay Willybach, her very own dear Willybach.

It had truly been a wonderful evening for her, an evening she knew she would remember all her life.

She had enjoyed the meal with its strange but delightful dishes, and that one glass of champagne she had been allowed in order to drink a toast to the radiant Leonie and dear, shy, proud Uncle Charles, still seemed to be bubbling pleasantly inside her.

It was an evening full of happiness for everyone.

Under the bed Willybach whimpered and stirred slightly. Fluff reached out her hand to reassure him.

"Gorwedd," she murmured, "Gorwedd!" Then she fell fast asleep.

THE END – ALMOST

An Endword and a Promise

If a book can have a Foreword an Endword may also be permitted. In this case an Endword seems to be necessary if all the loose ends are to be properly tied up, and a promise made for the future.

What has happened in the six months which have sped by since that happy evening at the Hilton Hotel?

Caradoc Evans has spent the time in a prison hospital. His memory is only slowly returning, and he has a stiff prison sentence to face.

Buss Frisby is back at Dartmoor, and his sister Lil is also in prison for her share in organising his escape. It is unlikely that these villains will give any trouble to anyone for a long time to come.

Uncle Charles and Leonie were married quietly in London with Fluff, as she puts it, "being a kind of bridesmaid". John took the photographs, and Mr and Mrs Jones came up from Dolgelley again for the occasion. Mrs Jones made the wedding cake.

The Frosts and the Carrs and, of course Willybach are now happily settled at White Hart Cottage, a converted Inn, which stands just on the outskirts of Merrihill, a village on the northern border of Hertfordshire. John and Fluff's school is within an easy cycle ride, and they have already made several friends in the village, and one enemy.

The enemy is the fat and ugly Mrs Crawthorne-Graham, who has a mole on her chin which sprouts thick black hairs. She lives in a cottage near the ruined church on the hill and keeps a cat. This black and satanic looking creature has been chased up a tree by an over-zealous Willybach, and this incident started the trouble.

"That woman," said Fluff to her friend Jennifer, as they leaned together over the vicarage gate and watched Mrs Crawthorne-Graham waddle up the road, "is a witch. I think we shall have a lot of trouble with her!"

And . . . But that's another story: and that's a promise!

THE END